BETRAYAL BY THE BAY

A TOURIST VISA MYSTERY
BOOK ONE

DAWN M. BACA

To my husband Jeremy,
I spent the first half of my life searching for you, and I'll
spend the rest of it grateful I found you.

To our cousins, Alan and Kyle,
Thank you for letting me include you in my stories, I hope I
did your characters justice.

Each morning we are born again.
What we do today is what matters most.
—Unknown

Paperback ISBN: 978-1-7329615-6-2
Editor: Roxx Tarantini
Cover: GetCovers.com
Chapter Image: Created in Canva

❀ Formatted with Vellum

CHAPTER
ONE

The crisp San Francisco air caressed Greer's cheeks, the tantalizing scent of freshly baked sourdough from a nearby bakery enveloping her. With trembling hands, she smoothed her meticulously chosen emerald-green sweater and charcoal slacks, a suit of armor against the vulnerability that threatened to engulf her.

After months of second-guessing her life choices, she'd finally settled on San Francisco. Not quite hiding—more like a tactical repositioning. *Tactical repositioning. Sure. If tactical meant hauling boxes up three flights of stairs while praying my Spanx don't give out.* The thought nearly made her chuckle. Who was she fooling? She was undeniably hiding.

"Time to get moving," she muttered, jaw set in determination.

After her divorce, the silence of her Denver house had grown unbearable. San Francisco wasn't just a change of scenery—it was her chance to trade that hollow quiet for something alive. Strolling down the sidewalk, her keen eyes darted from one architectural marvel to another. Grand Victorian houses stood tall and proud, their facades a sharp contrast to the sleek, contemporary buildings that lined the street—a perfect blend of the city's rich history and its constantly evolving present. The concrete under her feet offered a reassuring stability she hadn't experienced in months.

Each stride widened the gap between her, and Peter's suffocating shadow. As she pressed on, a cable car rumbled by, its bell chiming a cheerful melody. A smile broke across Greer's face, even as emotion clawed at her voice.

"I could certainly get used to that sound," she mused, though she'd probably never get used to the ticket prices.

At forty-nine, Greer found herself at a fork in the road—a new city, a new calling, a new existence.

All these changes were overwhelming. No more

being tied to a desk, answering emails, and scheduling meetings. No looming deadlines, no reports to submit, no wondering what meaning her life held. Just her charting her own course. The idea was both freeing and absolutely terrifying.

Pausing at the junction of Haight and Ashbury, Greer's freshly shorn chestnut curls—a defiant gesture against Peter's incessant admiration of her long hair—fluttered across her face in the crisp breeze. With a swift tuck of an errant strand behind her ear, she took in the lively storefronts and vivid murals gracing the Victorian edifices, each one more striking than the last.

A streak of cobalt blue slashed across the corner of a mural—too fresh, still wet. Greer frowned. It looked as if someone had tried to cover something up in a hurry. She took a photo, more out of habit than suspicion… but something about it nagged at her.

"No going back now," she whispered, cinching her bag tighter, her heart fluttering like a caged bird.

Her temples throbbed in rhythm with her steps. In the time she'd been stalking the streets of San Francisco, she'd memorized this neighborhood… and still felt like an imposter in her own story.

Greer had traversed countless cities, delving into their rich histories and hidden gems. But being the central character in her own life's plot twist felt far less glamorous. Her fingers ached for the comfort of her laptop, longing to transform this uncharted vulnerability into something polished and palatable.

She reached for her trusty leather notebook, hastily scribbling a thought about the neighborhood's eclectic vibe before slipping it back into her bag. Without thinking, her fingers brushed against the bare skin where her wedding ring once rested, the absence still palpable half a year later.

The weathered leather cover was a steadfast partner, its scuffed surface a silent witness to the adventures she'd experienced. It was easier that way. Ink on paper never asked for emotional investment or made vows, only to break them over a latte.

"Enough, Greer." Her voice wavered. "That chapter's over. Time to write the next."

If only life had a delete button to erase unwanted chapters. She had become a master at crafting flawless conclusions for her articles, so why couldn't she write one for herself?

The pain of her shattered marriage lurked beneath the surface—Peter's casual confession, how he'd discarded their twenty-five-year union with a flippant, "I'm just not in love with you anymore," as if commenting on the forecast. Greer forced it down, her fingernails biting into her palms. Despite the heartache, she refused to let it define her, determined to seize this chance and finally call the shots in her own life.

Each step defied the pull of everything trying to hold her back. For years, she'd witnessed the lives of others from a safe distance, an observer rather than a participant. Now, the spotlight was on her, and its intensity was overpowering.

A cluster of tourists rushed by, their lively banter yanking Greer from her musings. She remembered her own starry-eyed amazement when exploring unfamiliar places. A time when the world felt full of endless possibilities instead of jaded by disappointment.

She eyed their matching backpacks and crisp maps—tourists unburdened by what-ifs. Their carefree excitement stirred something raw and envious inside her.

"Sorry to bother you," she called out to a passerby, her voice slightly shaky, "but do you know a good spot for coffee around here?"

The stranger pointed up the street. "Groovy Brews, just a few blocks that way. Can't miss it."

"Appreciate it," Greer responded, a genuine smile growing, the sensation almost unfamiliar after so long. Her cheeks felt stiff from neglect.

As she continued walking, her thoughts raced with the promise of new beginnings, each stride a courageous leap into the unfamiliar.

This was precisely what she needed—a blank slate where no one saw her as the high-strung over-achiever with immaculate style, mingling perfectly at happy hour. In this city, she could redefine herself. Although she'd probably still be the one dragging friends to her place to watch history documentaries on movie night.

Greer felt a spark ignite within her. The burden of everyone's expectations faded with each step along the lively sidewalk.

Twenty-odd years of feigning interest in neighborhood gossip when she yearned to unravel the secrets of ancient civilizations. Two decades of swapping recipes and discussing the latest home decor trends while dreaming of far-off lands.

"No more pretending," Greer declared, her voice a quiet yet fierce promise to herself amidst the bustling city. "This is where I chase my passions."

As the fog lifted, revealing the majestic Golden Gate Bridge, Greer halted at the street corner, basking in the sunlight that danced across the bay. Her heart swelled with a long-forgotten sensation. The thrill of possibility.

She'd pored over countless images of this iconic view, but those online snapshots paled compared to the real thing.

"Pardon me," a voice broke through her thoughts. An elderly man holding a map approached, a quizzical expression on his face. "Do you know the way to Fisherman's Wharf?"

Perfect. First day in San Francisco and I'm already failing the entrance exam. San Francisco 1, Greer 0. Maybe I should invest in one of those fanny-pack maps.

Greer's cheeks warmed with embarrassment. "I apologize, sir. I just moved here myself. Landed a job at a travel magazine, believe it or not." The admission carried a mix of excitement and self-doubt.

The gentleman laughed good-naturedly. "Ah, it appears we're both starting new chapters! I wish you all the best in your new position."

She could almost hear her mother's disapproving tone. "Traipsing around the globe is hardly a respectable profession, Greer." *Respectable? Please.* She'd rather eat gas station sushi than sit through another church bake sale. If only her family could appreciate the accolades Greer had accumulated over the last year, not to mention that glorious moment when a popular food blogger shared her post on the flavors of East Asian cuisine.

Watching the man walk away, Greer felt a tug in her chest. The same one that had propelled her to this city after a lifetime of playing it safe. She was here to heed the call that had echoed within her since crafting her first tale at age twelve.

What if?

What if this was where she truly belonged, in the company of fellow adventurers and visionaries? What if those countless hours spent studying travel guides and mastering phrases in a multitude of tongues were more than just pipe dreams?

Squaring her shoulders, Greer forged ahead, her steps purposeful despite the butterflies in her stomach. The melodies of street performers and the tantalizing scents of global fare enveloped her, each one a reminder of the untold stories that had lain dormant in her journals for far too long. Stories that demanded to be shared with the world.

TWO

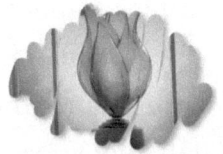

G reer's loafers clicked against the cobblestones as she delved further into the heart of Haight-Ashbury, a medley of vintage charm and bohemian spirit unfolding before her eyes. She drank in the eclectic storefronts, each one a portal to a different era or state of mind. A pang of restlessness stirred within her, a reminder that despite her newly nomadic lifestyle, she still yearned for a place to call home. It brought back memories of her first day at college, the empty dorm room a blank canvas waiting to be filled with new experiences. Now, Greer found herself in a similar position, ready to start a new chapter in her own life.

"Feels like a groovy time warp," she muttered,

notebook in hand. The battered journal had become her steady companion—always listening, never judging. She'd paused a moment to take in the surrounding area, and as her pen danced across the page, she captured snippets of the vibrant scene. Psychedelic murals that transported her back to her own youthful aspirations, the scent of incense wafting from crystal shops, reminiscent of her mother's signature fragrance, Sand and Sable, and street performers adorned with flower crowns, making her wonder if she'd waited too long to blossom into her true self.

Becoming a travel writer without a permanent address wasn't lost on Greer. She could already picture her sister's reaction if she caught wind of her current situation. She'd likely stage yet another well-meaning but misguided intervention, urging her to put down roots and settle down, as if a fixed address was the key to contentment.

Just as she turned the corner, a flash of orange caught her eye. There, perched regally on a nearby stoop, was a magnificent tabby cat. Its piercing gaze locked on her with an intensity that made her feel seen and understood for the first time in ages.

"Well, aren't you a sight for sore eyes?" Greer cooed, bending down to greet her new acquaintance. The cat's ears twitched. In a heartbeat, it bounded over, twining itself around her legs with a deep, rumbling purr. This unapologetic display of affection caught Greer off guard, and she blinked back unexpected tears.

With a soft chuckle, she reached down to stroke the cat. "You wouldn't happen to know of any vacant apartments in the area, would you? A cozy spot for a wandering soul, perhaps? Not like Zillow's been much help so far. Who'd have thought looking for rent-controlled with a side of emotional stability was going to be on my bingo card this year?"

Greer shuddered. Was it the soft breeze, or realizing she'd officially reached the point of conversing with random felines? At this rate, she'd be well on her way to becoming the neighborhood's resident eccentric, feeding pigeons in the park and rambling about government conspiracies. All she needed now was a shopping cart and a tinfoil hat to complete the look.

The tabby simply purred more insistently, nuzzling its face against her palm and offering a level of unconditional acceptance Greer hadn't experienced since bidding farewell to her previous life.

A shrill clang echoed from a nearby alley. Greer's head snapped up, heart skipping. Probably nothing—but the cat's tail puffed. She lingered a moment longer than she'd meant to, the silence pressing too tightly against her ribs. Then she walked on, telling herself it wasn't her business.

"Don't get any ideas, buddy," she warned. "I'm in no position to adopt a furry roommate. My budget's stretched thin enough as it is without adding a four-legged dependent to the mix."

Apartment hunting felt less daunting with the bold tabby at her heels. In a sea of strangers, the cat offered unexpected comfort—whiskers, fur, and all. For someone who prided herself on maintaining a safe emotional distance, Greer felt surprisingly attached to this charming stray. At this rate, she'd be signing up for dating apps and joining book clubs in no time.

Greer's fingers grasped at her unruly hair, the loose strands a frustrating reminder of her current predicament.

"Oh, for the love of..." she grumbled, fumbling for the hair tie on her wrist. As she watched the cat, the elastic band slipped from her fingers, bouncing onto the sidewalk. Perfect. As if juggling her wind-blown hair and apartment hunting wasn't enough of a challenge. *Great. Mugged by a cat. It would be fun explaining that to an insurance adjuster.* Bending to retrieve it, the tabby seized the opportunity, snatching the hair tie in its mouth and darting away.

The mischievous feline wove through the forest of legs, leaving Greer no choice but to give chase. Every rational fiber in her body screamed at her to turn back, to retreat to the safety of her hotel room and lose herself in crafting yet another article about tried-and-true tourist traps. But something deep within her propelled her forward.

Here she was, a forty-nine-year-old woman, chasing a kleptomaniac cat through the winding streets of San Francisco as if possessed. If she made it out of this impromptu adventure without a broken bone or a feature on the local news, it would be worth a mention in her next therapy session.

"You've got to be kidding me," Greer huffed, tightening her grip on the worn strap, breath catching in the cold air. When had she become this person, so reliant on careful planning and safety nets? The crisp wind picked up and tousled her curls, and for once she had to let them run wild, since she hadn't bothered to carry a second clip or band.

The tabby continued its relentless retreat; its orange tail a beacon guiding her through the crowds toward something uncharted. Was it running from her or leading her somewhere? Greer had penned countless blog posts encouraging others to trust their instincts. Maybe it was time she followed her own advice.

Her legs ached from the unexpected cardio, but a part of her thrived on the spontaneity, a feeling she'd been growing to appreciate since her safe and predictable life had been upended the previous year. Every day since had been a whirlwind of changes.

"This is not what I had in mind when I said I wanted to seize the day!" Greer panted, her earlier resolution coming back to haunt her. But really, what had she expected? A perfectly timed epiphany, neatly slotted between her morning coffee and afternoon tea? Her therapist would be thrilled, she mused wryly—finally embracing spontaneity, even if it meant chasing a cat through the city streets like a madwoman. She really had to start being more specific with her pep talks.

Without warning, the tabby veered into a narrow alley, its walls adorned with a riot of street art. Greer stumbled to a stop at the mouth of the alley, her lungs burning and her heart threatening to burst from her chest. The passage stretched out before her. Her pulse spiked—adrenaline or dread, she couldn't tell—but she stepped forward.

The primal warning that had tormented her for the past year now clawed at her mind, demanding attention. She'd seen her fair share of sketchy alleys to know better than this. And yet, here she was, trailing after a cat like some wide-eyed tourist, a far cry from the savvy woman she claimed to be.

Rooted to the spot, Greer couldn't escape the suspicion that the cat had guided her to this place for a purpose—but what that purpose could be, she hadn't the faintest idea. This wasn't some charming cultural discovery she could polish into prose. No amount of diplomatic phrasing or clever wordplay could transform this moment into something suitable for her readers' breakfast tables.

THREE

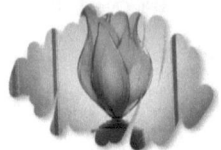

The kaleidoscopic graffiti swirled around her as Greer's footsteps pounded against the cracked pavement. She stopped short.

In front of her, a man lay sprawled on the ground, his body contorted like a broken marionette. A pool of blood spread beneath him, the bright crimson a stark contrast to his ashen face and the lively graffiti surrounding him.

This couldn't be real.

"Frack," Greer breathed, her heart pounding against her chest. She froze, torn between the instinct to help and the impulse to flee.

Something shifted at the far end of the alley. A shadow—gone before she could register it. Greer tensed. *Was someone still there? Watching?*

Her journalistic detachment shattered, all her hard-learned tricks for staying neutral in tough situations evaporating like mist under the sun. She reached for her notebook—then froze. Not this time. This wasn't a story. This was real.

The acrid reek of blood and waste stung her nose as she crept closer, her gaze darting around the alley. *Keep it together, Greer. You've got this.* But her body had other ideas—locked knees, lungs forgetting how to breathe.

Fifteen feet. That's all that stood between her and potentially ending up as front-page news herself. 'Globetrotting Journalist Finds Corpse in Alley.' Nope. 'Middle-Aged Woman Trips Over Crime Scene, Becomes Meme.' Definitely not. 'Intrepid Reporter Rescues Injured Man.' Better. If only she could convince her legs to move.

"Hello? Sir? Are you okay?" Greer's voice trembled as she drew nearer. Silence greeted her, broken only by faraway traffic and the frantic drumming of her own heart. The wet pavement seeped into her shoes, anchoring her to this waking nightmare she longed to escape.

Kneeling beside the man, Greer's hand quivered as she reached for his wrist, feeling for a pulse. That simple touch made it viscerally real. No longer a scene to report on from a comfortable distance.

This was worlds away from hosting cocktail parties and attending galas of the past. This was visceral, urgent, and utterly beyond her expertise.

"Come on, come on," she pleaded under her breath, straining to focus. Detachment warred with a swell of fierce compassion. Every fiber of her being yelled at her to scrutinize each detail, to file away every fact. But the coppery tang of blood shattered that illusion.

As Greer waited for any sign of life, a bevy of questions consumed her. Who was this guy? What on earth happened to him? And why, of all places, did it have to be in this vibrant alley she'd foolishly rushed into? So much for appreciating the artistic ambiance. Trust a furry little demon to guide her straight into a nightmare.

"Leave it to me to stumble ass-backwards into a story while house hunting," Greer grumbled, her go-to snark doing little to veil her skyrocketing panic. She mentally slapped herself for spiraling into tangents, a feeble attempt to outrun the dread threatening to swallow her whole.

Get it together, Greer.

Forty-nine years on this earth, and she'd avoided

witnessing death up close. Dear Goddess, please don't let today be the day that streak ends. All her life experiences meant jack squat right now—she was just another terrified bystander in an alley, praying she wasn't too late.

Relief crashed over her as she detected a thready, uneven rhythm beneath her touch. "Oh, thank heavens, he's still hanging on!" Greer blurted out, her voice quaking with a potent cocktail of solace and distress. Adrenaline-fueled fingers scrabbled for her phone, her typically deft movements rendered clumsy by the surge of stress hormones.

"911, what's the nature of your emergency?" The dispatcher's unruffled tone jarred against Greer's frenetic state of mind.

Greer barely recognized her own voice, the words spilling out as if spoken by a stranger—someone far more equipped to navigate this waking nightmare.

"There's a man bleeding out in the alley off Masonic, by the art gallery!" Greer's panicked words raced through the phone. "Send an ambulance, now!" She'd sounded like a caffeinated auctioneer. Hopefully, dispatch spoke "panicked tourist."

Sirens wailed in the distance as she ended the

call, the sound piercing the air like a battle cry. The once-vibrant graffiti now felt garish against the grim tableau at her feet, mocking her with its cheerful hues.

"Stay with me, okay?" Greer whispered to the unconscious man, her voice uncharacteristically tender. "You're going to be alright. Help's on the way."

An odd symbol caught her eye, spray-painted in fresh blue paint near the man. Cobalt blue. Just like the swipe she'd spotted near the mural earlier. A tremor rippled down her spine. She'd brushed it off, focused on the art. But now… now she wondered if that sound in the alley—the cat's puffed tail— meant more than she'd wanted to admit.

She hadn't missed a story.

She'd missed a warning.

Moments like this made her hand itch to reach for her pen.

The sirens reached a crescendo, painting the alley in lurid red and blue. The stench of her surroundings assaulted her senses, bile rising in her throat. Paramedics descended, a flurry of focused activity. Greer stumbled back, heart thundering, her mouth bone-dry. A life behind a desk had done nothing to prepare her for this.

"What happened?" a paramedic asked, loading the man onto a stretcher.

"No idea. Found him like this," Greer replied, marveling at her own composure. If only her high school debate coach could see her now. All that training, and here she was defending her innocence with barely clinging composure. "Is he going to make it?"

The question tasted bitter, a grim echo of that night in Denver, watching her friend being loaded into an ambulance. Helplessness settled over her like a lead shroud.

The paramedic's expression remained impassive. "We'll do our best. Anyone else around when you found him?"

"No, I don't think—" Greer's words caught in her throat as the gravity of the question hit her, her mind spinning with increasingly unsettling possibilities.

Freaking déjà vu. She'd promised herself never again. No more risky or dangerous situations.

It didn't matter what she told herself—somehow, she always circled back to watching history repeat itself with a vengeance. Greer clenched her fists, nails biting into her palms, the pain grounding her as the ambulance screamed into the night, leaving her with nothing but questions and the raw dread that her split-second delay might have sealed the man's fate.

CHAPTER

FOUR

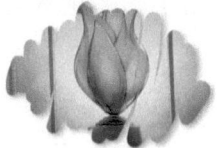

G reer stood staring at the alley wall, not really seeing the painted images. She reminded herself to stick to the facts and get out of there. Trouble always started this way. A single innocent question snowballing into another, until she was caught up in situations that would give her mother a heart attack. Not that a little maternal hand-wringing had ever deterred her.

Tires screeched as a cruiser swung to a stop. Two officers stepped out, their eyes hard, hands poised near their belts as they scanned the alley.

"Ma'am," said the taller one, his badge catching the streetlight. "Officer Reyes. This is Officer Chen.

You want to tell us why you're standing over a bleeding man in an alley?"

Greer swallowed, her throat dry. "I—I wasn't standing over him. As I was walking by, I heard something, and then I saw him lying there. I called 911 immediately."

Chen's pen scratched against his notepad, his eyes never leaving her face. "Just walking by, huh? In this part of town?"

"I'm a travel journalist," Greer said, forcing steadiness into her voice. "I was checking out the neighborhood for a piece."

Reyes's gaze flicked to her shoes, then to the smudge of blood on her slacks. "And you stopped in an alley because… what? Research?"

Greer's pulse hammered. "No—I followed a cat. It sounds ridiculous, but—hey, it had better street instincts than me."

Chen's brows rose. "A cat. That's your reason?"

The weight of their silence pressed on her. Terrific. She was about to become the cautionary tale in the next precinct PowerPoint: *How Not to Explain Yourself, Exhibit A.* Her instincts screamed to retreat, but she lifted her chin. Fake it 'til you make it, wasn't the motto of her life for no reason. "Yes.

And if I hadn't, that man might still be lying there with no one to help him."

Reyes stepped closer, voice low. "Or maybe you're hoping we'll believe that story." He pointed toward the ambulance, now pulling away. "Are you sure you've never seen him before? Not once?"

Greer shook her head. "Never."

Chen leaned in, his voice softer but sharper. "Because if we find out different—if your prints or your name come up tied to his—we'll be having a very different conversation downtown."

Reyes studied her for a long moment before finally nodding. "Don't leave the city, Ms...?"

"Caldwell," she said, her voice steadier than she felt.

"Ms. Caldwell," Reyes repeated, scribbling in his notebook.

Greer forced herself to nod, though her stomach twisted. They didn't believe her. Not entirely. And worse—she wasn't sure she believed herself for chasing a damn cat into this nightmare in the first place.

No doubt Mom would gloat, *"I warned you"* right about now, as if confining herself to sanitized, pre-packaged suburbia would magically render the world harmless. And if Mom really wanted to twist the knife, she'd probably suggest Greer look into settling down again. Safer hobbies like gardening. Less independence. But she'd tried that, and her life had still been turned into a pile of smoldering rubble.

She had staked her entire life on trusting her instincts. Right now, those instincts were telling her this was no ordinary mugging. Her logical mind told her not to jump to conclusions. But her gut wasn't speaking the same language.

Reyes gave a curt nod to Chen. "This way, Ms. Caldwell."

Greer hesitated, eyes darting back to the smear of cobalt blue on the wall and the last flash of the ambulance's taillights. She wanted to protest, to insist she wasn't finished looking, but Chen's hard stare left no room for argument.

They guided her down the alley, their boots crunching glass and gravel in a steady rhythm while hers skittered over the uneven pavement. The further she walked from the spot, the heavier her chest grew. It felt less like being dismissed and more like being escorted.

Behind the patrol car, the world had narrowed to a patch of cracked sidewalk and the chemical reek of flares burning at the perimeter. The flashing lights painted the buildings red and blue, strobing across the crowd of onlookers pressing in at the tape. Phones hovered high, recording.

On the other side of the barrier, the curious crowd craned to see her, whispers threading through the night. To them, she wasn't a bystander. She was part of the story now, tangled in it whether or not she wanted to be.

"Stay back," Chen ordered the crowd, as he lifted the yellow tape strung between two sawhorses. Once she was safely on the other side of the bright yellow crime scene tape, Officer Chen looked at Greer again. "We may need a follow-up statement. Here's my card."

Greer's throat constricted. "Am I a suspect?"

Reyes's eyes lingered on her, unreadable. "Not yet. But you're not cleared either. You were the only one here when we arrived. That makes you important. You'll need to come down to the station and give a complete statement tomorrow."

Important. The word landed like a stone in her gut.

She hugged herself against the night air, the cold biting through her sweater, reminding her she really needed to rethink the whole 'fashion over layers' thing. Every instinct told her to run—to vanish into the San Francisco streets like the tourists she'd passed earlier.

Reyes shot her one last, dismissive glance before turning away, already focused on the incoming reports crackling over his radio. A crime scene tech brushed past her, lugging a heavy case of equipment, the metal edges knocking against her arm as if to remind her she was in the way. The crowd, sensing the spectacle was finished, began to thin out —murmurs fading as phones lowered and curious faces slipped back into the night. The show was over, and she was no longer the center of attention. Yet the knot in her stomach told her this was only the beginning. As the sound of the ambulance's sirens dissipated, Greer remained off to the side in the alley, studying the murals for anything out of place. A shiver ran through her, the same unnerving sensation she'd experienced when she knew her life in Denver was over. The once-cheerful street art now seemed ominous, its bright colors and patterns hiding untold secrets. An electrifying blend of excitement and apprehension twisted in Greer's gut.

"There's more to this," she mumbled, fingertips itching to brush a faint symbol hidden in the mural. Terror and curiosity surged—this design wasn't random.

She stared at the blue mark. A symbol? A warning? Whatever it was—it hadn't been meant for her.

Greer pulled out her phone and snapped a series of photos of the wall art, acting as if she were staring at its screen; her thoughts whirling with endless possibilities. It might lead nowhere, or it could change everything. Another instance of her tenacious, some might say reckless, curiosity. Common sense dictated she let it go—hadn't her therapist warned her about this? "Greer, you're not responsible for righting every wrong." But she was mistaken. In her experience, every choice held the power to reshape reality.

She could practically hear her mother's condescending lecture ringing in her ears. As if caution and complacency had ever really worked. Certain moments required boldness, demanded a person obstinate enough to relentlessly pursue them.

"See something you like?" A startling voice shattered her concentration.

Greer silently cursed herself as she flinched, her muscles coiling with tension. So much for staying alert.

Looking over her shoulder, she found herself face-to-face with an older homeless man, his expression an intriguing mix of interest and suspicion. Her fight-or-flight instincts were warring within.

"Oh, just appreciating the artwork," she answered breezily, defaulting to her well-honed diplomatic persona. "I'm a travel journalist writing a piece on the city's street art culture."

The response flowed effortlessly, a skill she'd polished through countless miserable business dinners. It was almost funny how her social unease had morphed into an asset. Years of practice had taught her to cloak her nerves beneath a veneer of professionalism.

The man's eyes narrowed, skepticism etched on his features. "Pretty odd timing, don't you think? Considering what just happened here?"

Unease skittered down Greer's spine, but she brushed aside the instinct to bolt. "In my experience, the most compelling stories have a way of finding us when we least expect it," she remarked casually, holding his gaze with a sharp, assessing look of her own. "I don't suppose you have any insight into the incident?"

That carefully nonchalant approach had served Greer well in the past. People usually fell for her unassuming trophy wife routine or tipped their hand by reacting too aggressively.

Greer recognized the veiled threat, a familiar refrain she'd encountered with the "ladies who lunch" group that she'd avoided every chance she got. Apparently, these types never learned that intimidation only fueled her determination.

As the stranger disappeared down the alley into the shadows, Greer's heart thundered in her chest. She sagged against the chilly brick wall, her trembling fingers seeking stability on the gritty surface. Perhaps her reckless curiosity was a result of a life playing it safe, a stubborn defect that reared its head when the ashes cooled. The tantalizing lure of unraveling this enigma, of potentially making a difference, overpowered her self-preservation.

"Well, well, looks like you've stumbled onto a pretty big scoop. Just don't get yourself killed in the process," Greer muttered, the words tasting sour on her tongue, a vow she couldn't guarantee. The sarcastic quip hung in the air, a jab at her crumbling professionalism. When had she started talking to herself in creepy alleys? Her therapist would have a field day with this.

Casting a final glance at the cryptic symbolism on the wall, Greer exited the alley, her mind filled with unanswered questions and intriguing possibilities. Her originally planned street art article would have to be shelved. Something sinister was in this city, a story she hadn't expected to be a part of. The kind of exposé that could catapult a journalism career or cut it brutally short. Since when did she decide to pursue mysteries? Or crime reporting? With a surprised huff, she steeled herself for the arduous path ahead, surprised to find the uncertainty more exhilarating than terrifying. Maybe, just maybe, this time would be different.

"Alright, Greer, time to put that insatiable curiosity to work," she thought, quickening her stride as she reached the main street. "There's a devil of a story waiting to be uncovered, and you're in just the position to do it."

Determination steeled her spine even as the breeze carried a silent warning. Her fingers ached for her laptop—facts, order, control—but this story wouldn't come that easily.

FIVE

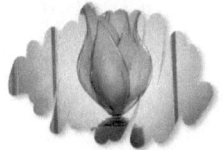

Police tape fluttered in the breeze as Greer crossed the road, nearing the alley where she'd discovered the body just a week ago. Memories of that afternoon haunted her, fragments of the scene invading her thoughts—the coppery tang of blood, the unnerving quiet. She'd pored over every detail, desperate for answers that eluded her. A flash of teal and gold caught her eye—there he was, alive and well, studying a gallery window with an intensity that gave her pause. Relief and unease intertwined as she watched him, unharmed and breathing.

The emerald stud in his ear caught the morning light as he tilted his head. Greer's instinct pinged. Behind him, someone lingered in the glass's reflection. A man in a charcoal hoodie, watching—but gone when she blinked again. His stance seemed off-kilter, like a picture frame not quite straight. The stiffness in his shoulders under the blue-green colored silk hinted at more than a simple interest in the artwork. She recognized that posture—the subtle angle of someone hunting for something deeper.

Greer's gaze was drawn to the man's image reflected in the gallery window. The hint of a story pulled at her thoughts. She didn't reach for the notebook tucked into her bag. Yet. But her fingers itched with questions.

He frowned as he examined whatever was behind the glass. The mix of longing and determination on his face resonated with her. It was too familiar, mirroring her own expression when her mind was a jumble of confusion.

Torn between her reflex to keep her distance and her usual inquisitiveness, Greer hesitated. Social unease battled with journalistic drive. Walking away, maintaining her normally solid walls, would be the prudent choice. Prudent, boring, and about as satisfying as a kale smoothie. But then again, when had taking the easy road worked out for her? She fiddled with the edge of her jacket, an anxious habit she'd never quite kicked. The recent chaos had shaken her, but the promise of answers was impossible to ignore. And the man mere steps away, with his daring fashion and contemplative demeanor, was undeniably intriguing.

Car fumes mixed with the sweet scent of spring blossoms as she drew closer, her practical running shoes silent on the cracked sidewalk. Her thoughts raced with each step. This could lead nowhere—or everywhere. The line between recklessness and revelation often hinged on moments like this.

As she approached the window, the art on display came into sharp focus—abstract works that pulsed with energy and passion, all bold strokes and barely contained chaos.

"Incredible pieces," Greer commented, her steady voice masking her inner chaos as she stepped up beside him.

The man started, his adorned hand clutching his chest. A hint of discomfort flashed across his features before he masked it with a smile.

"Darling, you nearly gave me a coronary!" His lilting laugh sounded forced, his gaze darting to the road behind her.

Coronary? Oh please. She barely startled him. If

she was going to be accused of something, overzealous greeter wasn't what she'd hoped for.

"Alan Caputo, gallery owner and art aficionado, at your service."

"Greer Caldwell. I found you in the alley." The words felt foreign in her mouth, like dialogue from someone else's script.

"Well, well, if it isn't my guardian angel!" Alan's grin widened, but didn't seem to reach his eyes as his fingers drummed a restless rhythm against his thigh. "I've been dying to thank you properly. How about a little VIP tour? I've got some absolute treasures squirreled away, not quite ready for the main showroom."

Her curiosity pressed her forward. Too late to back out now. Cue ominous music. She nodded— too quickly. *Dagnabbit, Greer.*

Greer lingered near the entrance, hands in jacket pockets, shoulders slightly hunched—bracing, maybe, against a space that whispered permanence when her life felt anything but.

Alan stood nearby, casually leaning against a pedestal, though his sharp eyes betrayed something heavier.

"I don't know how to thank you," he said. "If

you hadn't been there…" He stopped, palms pressed together like he was holding back the rest. His eyes dropped, then found hers again. "I don't want to finish that sentence."

Greer offered a faint smile. "I wasn't supposed to be there. I was following a cat."

That startled a laugh—short but real. His shoulders relaxed.

"A cat?"

"Mm-hm." She rocked back on her heels. "Scruffy little thing. Orange, wild tail. Stole my hair tie and ran. I followed him across the street, into the alley. And then there you were—flat out on the ground. Not moving." Her throat tightened. "I didn't let myself finish that thought either. I just called 911."

Alan exhaled slowly. "The stars must've sent that cat. Or you. Or both. It was close. Too close."

She crossed her arms, uneasy under the weight of his gratitude. And yet—something about being here with him, in this space, steadied her more than it should've.

"I'm just glad I didn't ignore it," she murmured.

Alan nodded.

A quiet stretched between them. Not awkward,

just... full. Her gaze drifted to a painting across the room—indigo crashing into white, like waves against sky. She could get lost in that. Easier than facing the truth: new city, no safety net, dwindling funds.

"Anyway, let me show you around," Alan said as he led her through the gallery, rhapsodizing about brushstrokes and color theory. His infectious zeal drew Greer in. Yet, an undercurrent of unease threaded through his movements, as if he were an understudy thrust into the spotlight unprepared.

Something about Alan's fervor felt forced, his hands flitting between canvases, his tone pitching up and down with artificial excitement.

Two men walked into the gallery together. A handsome man who clearly took great care in his appearance, a little too much if she was being honest. For some reason, he reminded her a little of the ladies who lunched crowd she'd known in Denver. Next to him strode a distinguished, silver-fox type in a navy suit, exuding the easy arrogance of someone who took no prisoners. The older man extended a hand, and Alan seized it, his own grasp a tad overenthusiastic, like a kid playing dress-up in his dad's clothes. While they were probably close in age, based on the creases across their faces and the crepe-like skin on their hands, Alan was clearly fighting the aging process, with his dark and perfectly styled hair, while the other man appeared to have submitted to its inevitability. The man's perfectly tailored threads likely cost more than her ex-husband made in a month. She'd crossed paths with enough suits to know the type. All ego and entitlement.

"Alan! Wanted to give you a heads up. As I mentioned to Marco here, my crew got that rear entrance sorted, new steel door and all." The man's tone was breezy, but his eyes were distant.

"Thank you, Charles, for having my back." Alan's strained smile didn't quite reach his eyes.

"Of course. Anyway, didn't mean to crash your little chat here." The stranger barely acknowledged Greer.

The way he sized her up, dismissive and unim-pressed, rankled her. He looked at her the way sommeliers looked at boxed wine. There were far too many men like him. "How rude of me. Charles Henderson, meet Greer Caldwell, the lady who came to my rescue that night."

Charles clasped Greer's hand, his touch featherlight compared to the death grip he'd given Alan. There was something in his stare, a shrewd, appraising glint that raised her hackles.

"And this other gentleman is Marco, the assistant curator of the gallery. Not much happens without his input."

Marco simply smiled and nodded, his hands clasped behind his back. He stepped away from them, heading to the front of the gallery, where someone was looking into the window from the street.

"Well, I'll leave you two to it. Just wanted to make sure the crew cleaned up." With a smile, Charles sauntered out, towards the back of the gallery, with the confidence of a man who owned the world.

She watched him vanish into the shadows, her mind already cataloging details for later analysis. It brought back the effort of dealing with Peter's colleagues and the way she'd always longed for a shower afterward.

Alan's voice pulled her back from her internal musings.

"...Odd occurrences have been plaguing this place recently," Alan admitted, his voice wavering as he twisted his hands together. "Valuables vanishing from secure displays, documents going missing, strange noises echoing through the halls at night." His eyes darted around the deserted gallery, as if the weight of his words was bearing down on him. "And just days before my... attack... a priceless miniature disappeared without a trace."

"Have you reported it?"

"The police think I'm being paranoid." Alan's fingers trembled as he adjusted his collar. "But something's wrong here, Greer. I can feel it in my bones."

She studied his face, noting the worry lines around his eyes, the way his mouth twitched with suppressed fear. "When do these incidents usually occur?"

"Weekends, especially after events. There was this couple last Saturday, asking oddly specific questions about our security..." He trailed off, watching her. "You're not just being polite, are you? You're actually interested?"

Her pulse quickened with familiar anticipation. This wasn't in her comfort zone, but the mystery beckoned just the same. And if mysteries came with Yelp reviews, this one would be rated 'sketchy but irresistible.' And Alan needed her. The realization struck her with surprising force.

That old steel door slammed shut—the same one Peter's exit had forged. Her breath hitched before she could stop it.

The bitter taste of betrayal rose in her throat, sharp and acrid as ever. A year later, and she still couldn't shake how efficiently he'd dismantled everything she'd believed about their relationship. About herself.

One step at a time. She reminded herself, forcing her attention back to Alan's words. For now, she'd listen, observe, and see where this unexpected encounter might lead. Greer knew she wasn't imagining things.

The silence descended again, not an uncomfortable tension, just a muted quiet in the air around them as he focused on a painting on the wall in front of them.

"So, what's got you so enraptured with this piece? Is it some avant-garde masterpiece or a scandalously abstract work of genius?"

Alan tilted his head, a thoughtful expression on his face. "You know, it's actually quite a traditional painting—a landscape of the Bay Area from the turn of the century. I'm just trying to ensure it's showcased in the best possible light. There's something captivating about the way the artist captured the luminescence…"

Her fingers itched for her notebook, muscle memory from countless interviews kicking in. Strange how comfort could be found in the motions of work, even when everything else felt sideways.

CHAPTER
SIX

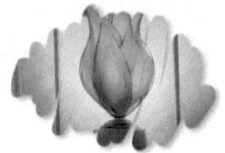

Greer moved closer to the display, studying the artwork through the glass. The painting radiated with the warm glow of the golden hour, that fleeting moment when the world seems to pause between day and night. A pang of familiarity struck her—it echoed the same liminal space she'd found herself in since the divorce, suspended between her past and an uncertain future.

"I can see why it caught your eye. It's as if the artist bottled up that magical instant just before the sun dips below the horizon. The way the light dances across the water's surface…"

"Yes, precisely!" Alan's face lit up with enthusiasm, his rings catching the light as he gestured animatedly. "I must say, Greer, you have a keen eye for art appreciation."

She almost snorted at that. Her knowledge of art began and ended with what looked good on magazine covers. But writing her blog had taught her to notice details, to piece together the subtle nuances that made a story worth telling.

"Well, in my line of work, it pays to examine things from every angle." The air hung heavy with the commingled scents of aged canvas and crisp lemon polish. "Often, the most crucial clues are hidden in plain sight, just waiting to be discovered."

Alan's bravado faltered, a glimmer of raw vulnerability shining through his polished exterior. "This gallery... it's everything to me. I can't let whatever's going on here jeopardize that." He paused, his fingers nervously tapping against the display case. "I don't suppose you'd be interested in putting your investigative skills to work here? Strictly off the record, of course."

Her pulse quickened at the suggestion. The rational part of her brain screamed this wasn't her problem—she wrote about restaurant openings, and cultural festivals, not crimes and art gallery mysteries. And yet...

A laugh escaped Greer's lips as she brushed an

errant curl from her face. "Investigative skills? Alan, I'm hardly Sherlock Holmes. And trust me, I'm certainly no art aficionado."

"Ah, but that's where you're wrong," Alan countered with a playful grin. "True expertise comes from the heart, not some stuffy academic credential. And you, darling, have got passion under that calm veneer."

Self-doubt crept in, that nagging voice questioning every achievement she'd earned. Her blogs spoke for themselves, didn't they?

A flicker of warmth slipped through her guard. Somehow, she was trading quips with Alan like they'd known each other for years.

She shifted her stance, adjusting the strap of her messenger bag—her security blanket in social situations. The easy rapport with Alan felt foreign, yet oddly natural. She couldn't remember when she had relaxed her vigilance like this.

"I've gotta say," Alan confessed, his voice low and sincere, "running into you today? Best thing that's happened all week. It's a relief to have someone who actually gets it, you know?"

The genuine warmth in his words threatened to melt her practiced detachment. God, she was rusty at this friendship thing.

A genuine smile played at the corners of Greer's mouth. "I know what you mean," she agreed. "It's been an enlightening encounter, to say the least."

One of Alan's eyebrows quirked upward, a silent question.

Panic fluttered in her chest. She could retreat now, stick to safe topics like brush strokes and color theory. But something about Alan's openness made her want to be brave.

Greer wavered, then decided to take a chance. Tracing her finger along the cool glass of the display, she was reminded of the day she'd slipped off her wedding band for good, the metal as icy as her heart had felt. She hesitated, her past making trust harder than she wanted to admit. "Opening up, letting people in… it's never been my strong suit. Heck, I don't even share my Netflix password," she admitted with a vague gesture between them. "Especially after the nightmare of my divorce."

Alan's face softened, understanding shining in his eyes like sunlight through honey. "I'm sorry. Change is hard."

The sympathy in his voice made her skin prickle. She'd rather endure an overly opinionated camel on a beach walk than discuss her failed marriage. But here she was, voluntarily bringing it up. Maybe she was getting soft.

She swallowed hard, eyes fixed on the window display. "It was brutal. Makes it hard to take that leap of faith."

"I can only imagine," Alan murmured, his tone laced with empathy. "But if you ask me? I think you're handling it with incredible grace."

She almost snorted. *Grace?* She'd tripped over three cobblestones on the way here. If that was grace, she was a ballerina. More like stubborn survival. She'd thrown herself into work before realizing she had nothing left to give the company she'd slaved at for over five years. A mini-midlife crisis, her mother had accused. But whatever it was, it drove her to walk away from that life and not look back. Maybe that counted as grace, in its own way.

They stood in companionable silence, the kind that feels both terrifying and safe, before Alan spoke again. "Change is hard, but necessary. You know, the gallery's been in my family for three generations. My grandfather started it back in the '40s."

Greer's curiosity piqued. "Really? That's impressive."

Alan's eyes took on a faraway look, his shoulders softening as if releasing a weight. "Yeah, he was quite a character. I remember sitting in his studio when I was seven, surrounded by the smell of oil paints and coffee. He'd tell me stories about smuggling art out of Europe during the war. Never could tell if they were true or just tall tales, but the way his voice would crack when he described saving certain pieces…" Alan swallowed hard.

Alan's memories pressed against her chest like a weight. Family legacies left her feeling like an outsider looking in through frosted glass. Close enough to see the shapes of what she'd missed, but never touching the warmth within.

"Wow," Greer said, her chest aching with unexpected recognition. "That must have been something."

She hadn't planned to sound wistful. Still, she'd slipped into someone else's story—like a tourist forgetting to pack for rain.

"It was," Alan said, his voice barely above a whisper. "He passed away when I was at college. Sometimes I worry I'm not living up to his legacy. That I'm just… pretending to be what he was."

His confession stirred something deep inside her. That familiar ache of trying to measure up to impossible standards. How many times had she stared at her published articles, picking apart every word choice, wondering if she deserved the byline?

The raw honesty in his admission made Greer's hands tremble. She curled them into fists, fighting the temptation to reach out. "I'm sure he'd be proud of you, Alan. The gallery looks amazing."

Alan gave her a grateful smile that reached past her careful defenses. "Thanks, Greer. That means a lot."

She should redirect the conversation, maintain professional boundaries. But Alan's openness had dissolved her usual protocols, like rain washing away carefully drawn lines in the sand.

Greer wanted to know more, even as she wrestled with the desire to keep her distance. Keeping conversations safely confined to meaningless small talk was her superpower. Yet here was Alan, casually dismantling her defenses with nothing more than honest words and genuine emotion.

Greer watched as Alan's eyes lit up, his hands gesturing animatedly as he described a new exhibit he was planning. "It's a showcase of emerging local artists blending traditional Art Deco and contemporary realism."

His passion was infectious, and Greer nodded along, captivated by his enthusiasm, though she half-expected him to break into jazz hands at any second. Something inside her chest thawed, like spring's first warm day. "That sounds incredible, Alan. The way you talk about art… it's like you breathe life into it."

Perhaps this was why she traveled. To find moments like these, when someone's passion illuminated the world in unexpected ways. When did she become so afraid of letting people in? *Peter*. The name reminded her that life could change in an instant.

Alan's cheeks flushed slightly at the compliment, his hand moving to rub the back of his neck. "It's more than just paintings on a wall, you know? Each piece tells a story, capturing a moment in time. I want people to feel that when they walk into the gallery. To feel less… alone."

A strange warmth bloomed in her chest, catching her off guard. She smiled, despite the gravity of the situation, despite the way her heart hammered against her ribs like a warning.

What are you getting yourself into, Greer? She scolded herself, shaking her head. Her heart filled with conflicting emotions, each one sharp as broken glass. A small voice of caution whispered reminders of past hurts and the dangers of getting too close.

It's just a friendship, Greer reassured herself, even as her heart warmed at Alan's infectious laugh. And a potential story. Nothing more. The lie tasted bitter on her tongue.

As she stood there watching Alan continue to glance around his gallery, she couldn't shake the feeling that something significant was shifting in her life. The walls of her carefully constructed independence seemed to crack, letting in a little light she wasn't sure she was ready to face.

Behind them, a floorboard creaked. They both turned, but the gallery remained empty—except for a familiar orange tabby cat sitting primly in the doorway, watching them. Greer couldn't help but wonder what secrets the orange tabby cat held in its knowing gaze.

CHAPTER
SEVEN

The fading daylight spilled through the Bayside Art Collective's windows, casting long shadows across the priceless artworks. The hair on Greer's neck prickled. Years of high-society events hadn't taught her how to belong, and she'd take a remote beach over this posturing any day.

"Just wait until you see it in all its scandalous glory, darling," Alan enthused, his vintage rings catching the light again as he gestured dramatically. "The raw, edgy way Carlos Martinez captured San Francisco's seamy side in those oil paintings—it's positively wicked! But between you and me," he leaned closer, lowering his voice conspiratorially,

"I'm not entirely convinced he painted them himself."

Something in Alan's tone set off alarms in her mind. In all her years, she'd never known anyone to doubt an artist's credibility.

Greer's curiosity piqued. "Really? What makes you say that?" Her gaze lingered on the signature at the bottom of a nearby canvas—Martinez, but shaky, like it had been added as an afterthought. Something about it felt… off.

Alan watched her—cautiously, thoughtfully.

"So," he asked, clearing his throat, "did you ever find what you were looking for that day?"

She laughed, the sound light but tinged with resignation.

"An apartment. And I've looked. And looked. But everything even remotely livable is miles out of my budget. I'm rethinking my life choices, honestly."

Alan rubbed his jaw, the corners of his mouth tugging downward in consideration. He was about to speak when the gallery door nudged open with a faint creak. An orange cloud sauntered inside, tail high, like it owned the place, purring without preamble.

Greer blinked, then laughed as the cat made a

beeline for her, winding around her legs with shameless affection. She crouched to stroke his back. He purred, loud and immediate.

"You again!" Greer laughed. "If I didn't know better, I'd think you've been stalking me?"

"There you are, Phoenix!" Alan's earlier unease seemed to vanish as he greeted the cat warmly. "Greer, our resident art critic, obviously likes you."

Greer quirked an eyebrow. "Yours?"

He shook his head. "Stray. Started showing up a few weeks ago, bold as brass. He was chewing on a postcard of Arizona. So, I started calling him Phoenix. I've been leaving food out. Seems to have nine lives." His gaze shifted from the cat to her, something sparking behind his eyes. "I guess he led you to me, too."

Greer laughed under her breath, scratching under Phoenix's chin. "I thought cats were supposed to be aloof and mysterious. This little guy's determined to shatter that myth."

"Face it, darling." Alan chuckled. "The cat distribution system has activated. You've been officially claimed. Time to lean into your new identity as a crazy cat lady."

Greer rolled her eyes. "Crazy cat lady? Please. I

don't even qualify for starter-level eccentric yet. Give me five more scarves and a crystal ball."

Phoenix's ears flicked toward the hallway, his body going still. Greer paused mid-stroke. Nothing moved, but the air shifted—like they weren't alone.

"Sometimes, my dear, the most unexpected connections are the ones that change everything," he said, twisting one of his rings round and round, a telltale sign of his nerves. Not so different from her own anxious habit of picking at her cuticles until they bled.

Greer's muscles stiffened at Alan's keen observation. Already, she could feel her guard slamming back into place, each inhale and exhale tightly controlled. This was exactly why she stuck to writing about places, not people.

Alan's silence made her look up. Then, with the same directness that had carried through his gratitude, he said, "The apartment upstairs has a spare room. It's nothing fancy, but it's private. I'd rent it out if you were interested. And it seems Phoenix has already decided you belong here." He gestured grandly at the tabby happily purring at Greer's ankles.

Greer's BS detector pinged. Spare room, cat included? Sounded like Craigslist—minus the ax-murderer vibe. Hopefully… Seriously, who could afford a place with a spare bedroom in this city? In her experience, offers that seemed too good to be true usually came with a hefty price tag. Still, the mere thought of spending one more night in that dingy motel, with its questionable stains and sketchy plumbing, made her want to scream bloody murder into her lumpy pillow. She'd been searching for weeks for a safe place to land, but nothing had come close to her limited budget.

Her recent voluntary isolation had drilled some hard truths about trust into her skull. Namely, that it was a luxury she couldn't afford. Yet, Alan's proposal called to her like a siren song. She'd built a career on reading between the lines, deciphering hidden meanings and backhanded subtleties. But now, faced with the simple act of accepting help, she was paralyzed.

She tucked her hair behind one ear, stalling. "We don't even know each other."

"True," Alan said. "But you found me when I couldn't help myself. That counts for something." He nodded toward the cat. "And sometimes… the right people cross paths when they need to."

She kept stroking Phoenix, grounding herself in the vibration of his purr.

"Yeah," she said softly. "I believe that."

They stood in the golden quiet—man, woman, and cat—stitched together by luck and something more elusive.

Still. Saying yes? Too much, too fast.

Alan must've read it on her face. He lifted his hands, palms out. "You don't have to decide. Just... come see it. No pressure. No strings."

Relief loosened something in her chest.

"Hmm." She glanced at Phoenix at her feet, utterly at ease.

"Oh, come on," Alan cajoled, sauntering towards a nondescript door tucked away in the back of the gallery. "If nothing else, the view of Haight-Ashbury alone is worth the price of admission."

Greer had built a solid blog following by encouraging her readers to embrace the unknown, to step outside their comfort zones. Now, faced with the prospect of shared living quarters, she found herself on the verge of a full-blown panic attack. The irony was almost laughable—if she managed to survive this experience, it would make one heck of a story for her next blog.

As she followed Alan up the cramped staircase, her fingers trembling slightly on the handrail, Phoenix darted ahead like a miniature orange bodyguard. Greer couldn't shake the sneaking suspicion she was about to get herself entangled in something far more complex than a simple room-mate situation.

"Behold, my not-so-modest digs!" Alan declared, flinging open the door at the top of the stairs with a flourish.

The apartment was an all-out assault on the senses. Luxurious Persian rugs blanketed the floors, the walls adorned with paintings that probably cost more than Peter's entire family's net worth, and crystals sparkling in the fading daylight. The fragrance of sandalwood mingled with the aroma of recently brewed coffee. But it was the massive abstract canvas dominating the living room that truly captured Greer's attention. A tempestuous sea of blues and grays that seemed to mirror the chaos within her own heart. The signature in the corner appeared to shimmer strangely in the waning light.

The swirling brushstrokes called to something deep inside her, an aching desire she couldn't put a name to. It reminded her of all the exotic alleyways she'd explored so far, seeking tales that would carry her readers far beyond the limits of their everyday lives. This place exuded that same irresistible allure.

"This is…" Greer began, struggling to find the

right words as the painting stirred something profound within her soul.

"Stupendous? Astounding? The pinnacle of bohemian chic?" Alan offered, his eyes twinkling with mischief.

Greer shook her head, a wry grin tugging at the corners of her mouth. Leave it to Alan to have the perfect quip at the ready. After years of painting vivid word pictures of far-off lands, she found herself at a loss in this quirky haven.

She chuckled as the tension in her shoulders dissipated. "I was leaning more towards 'mind-boggling,' but your suggestions are growing on me."

The vise-like grip around her heart loosened. This vibrant space was a world away from the soul-less townhouse she'd left behind, with his oppressive, quiet, and disapproving family always underfoot. Here, the air hummed with endless possibilities.

Greer hovered on the edge of something new—part terror, part thrill. The kind of plunge she hadn't taken in years.

Alan spun to face her, his movements imbued with theatrical flair. He gestured at the room like Vanna White on espresso. "So, what's the scoop, doll? Ready to be my spectacular new roomie?"

EIGHT

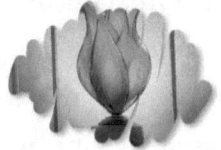

Greer paused, a familiar unease constricting her chest.

"Alan, I appreciate the offer, really. But..." She fiddled with a lock of hair, an old tell whenever she felt she was imposing. "What if I screw up this job? What if I can't return the favor? I've worked hard not to be in anyone's debt."

"Nonsense!" Alan cut in. "C'mon, we're pals, aren't we? Pals have each other's backs."

Sure. If pals came with matching coffee mugs and the occasional nervous breakdown. Greer bit back a smile, but something in his eyes made her pause—like he was offering more than just a place to crash. Like he needed someone to watch his back.

"You've already been there for me. Let me return the favor. Besides, imagine the juicy art scene scoops you'll get for your pieces."

The offer felt like a new jacket, mildly ill-fitting but somehow right. Greer grinned. She felt secure here. The burden riding her since arriving started melting away, like frost in the morning sun. The open room's imaginative vibe was palpable too— rays pouring through the high panes, illuminating flecks swirling like micro-galaxies.

She ought to scrawl this in her diary, under 'Rash Calls That May Pan Out.' Sadly, the section was barren.

"Okay," she relented. "Let's do this." *Heaven help me, I'm moving in with a stranger and a cat. This has cheesy Hallmark movie written all over it.*

Alan whooped joyfully. "Fantastic! *Mi casa es su casa*, girl."

Greer chuckled, *'home'* snagging her gullet like a sweet barb. It coiled in her mind, an unknown flavor she couldn't pin. As bizarre as it sounded, it was tempting.

"Methinks stuff's gonna get wild 'round these parts." Greer joked. It evoked her Gran's caution— someone treading your future tomb, she'd quip. A bygone notion from a lady convinced hunches hit the flesh prior to the noggin.

A shiver tingled down Greer's spine, but she shook it off. Gran's old superstitions had no place in her jet-setting life. She'd explored ancient ruins and remote villages, witnessing wonders that defied explanation. Still, a niggling doubt lingered.

Phoenix's graceful leap onto the vintage dresser pulled her from her thoughts. He surveyed his domain with regal satisfaction.

"Guess I'm more of a cat person than I realized," Greer mused, memories of her empty childhood resurfacing. *Why do I feel like my therapist would add 'feline co-dependence' to my file if she could see me now?*

Phoenix rolled over, offering his spotted tummy for a rub. Greer obliged, marveling at his silky fur and the rumbling purr that vibrated through her palm.

Alan leaned in, his eyes meeting hers with a mix of interest and gentle concern. "So, dish. That new gig at Epic Destinations—what wild and wonderful stuff are you hunting down?"

Greer felt a thrill of excitement tempered by self-doubt.

"Buenos Aires has this insane street art scene!

There's a mural in La Boca that blew my mind. It captures the barrio's complete history in this explosion of color and symbolism." Her voice caught. "Reminds me of the stories I read as a kid, before… Anyway, it's raw and real, and I've never seen anything like it. Pitched it to my new boss, but…" She trailed off, suddenly unsure if she was ready for this leap.

Alan's eyes sparkled with enthusiasm. "No kidding? That Argentinian showcase was mind-blowing! The way those artists wielded color like a weapon; it was pure genius."

Greer's bohemian instincts kicked into high gear, her mind already weaving together the threads of a killer story. Exploring the vibrant intersection of Buenos Aires street art and San Francisco's cutting-edge scene? Her readers would flip.

"Seriously? I've gotta hear more!" Greer leaned in, her hand unconsciously reaching for the battered notebook that never left her side. "This could be the angle I've been searching for."

The thrill of the chase, the adrenaline rush of a story begging to be told—this was what made Greer feel truly alive. But with the excitement came a twinge of anxiety, the fear of falling short.

As they traded tales of daring artists and under-ground galleries, Greer felt a rare sense of connection, as if a missing puzzle piece had slid into place. Alan's infectious passion mirrored her own, igniting a spark she thought had long since fizzled out.

Greer couldn't remember the last time she'd felt this at peace. It was like standing on the edge of a cliff, unsure whether to jump into the ocean or retreat to solid ground.

Her attention roamed over the riot of color and texture that seemed to mirror Alan's exuberant spirit. Each painting, each quirky knick-knack, held a story waiting to be unlocked. His main room was just so beautifully eclectic, yet it blended in such a way to not seem cluttered.

A small, faded photo caught her eye, tucked into the frame of an antique mirror. Two giggling kids, sandy and sunburned, their grins wide and carefree. The image hit Greer like a punch to the gut, dredging up memories of happier days—before she'd locked them away, determined to never look back.

Greer wrenched her focus back to the present, resisting the undertow of memories threatening to drag her under. Keep moving forward. That was her mantra. Always chasing the next story, the next adventure. It was the only foolproof defense she'd discovered against the lure of her past.

"It's crazy," she marveled, fingers absently tracing the faded scar on her palm, a nervous tic she'd never quite shaken. "I never imagined I'd stumble across a place in San Francisco that felt so fiercely electric."

"Ah, that's the Haight for you, sweetheart." Alan's eyes twinkled with mischief. "It has a way of getting into your bloodstream."

Normally, the casual term of endearment would have raised Greer's hackles—she was a master at deflecting such over-familiarity. But to her surprise, she found herself biting back a grin. *Great. Sounds like an artistic blood parasite.*

Greer hummed in agreement, her fingers idly stroking Phoenix's silky fur as he curled up in a ball at her hand. The steady thrum of his purr called to mind the scruffy street cat she'd fed throughout high school—the sole friend she'd permitted herself during those lonely years. "No wonder you're so smitten with this place. Every nook and cranny seems bursting with untold tales."

Alan leaned in, a conspiratorial glint in his eye. "Just wait 'til you experience the Haight Street Fair. It's pure, unadulterated chaos. In the most glorious way imaginable."

"Oh, I've heard the legends!" Greer's eyes sparkled with anticipation, then dimmed slightly. "I went to a street festival in Denver once, ages ago. I was supposed to meet up with a friend, but she bailed on me. Ended up roaming around solo for hours, trying to convince myself I was having the time of my life." She ducked her head, startled by her own candor.

The confession hung in the air, making Greer feel strangely vulnerable, as if she'd unintentionally let slip too much. Classic Greer move, spilling her guts to the first person who showed a glimmer of authentic interest. She'd spent years honing the skill of holding people at arm's length, keeping things strictly impersonal. And now here she was, unloading her life's letdowns on her new roomie like it was some kind of therapy session.

"Trust me, darling, you won't be flying solo at the fair," Alan reassured her with a playful wink. "Stick with me, and I'll make sure you're rubbing elbows with the crème de la crème of the Haight's artistic elite. We'll paint the town red together!"

The casual intimacy of his words sent a frisson of warmth through Greer, chasing away the chill of past disappointments. When was the last time someone had gone out of their way to include her, to make her feel like she belonged? Certainly not her husband or his family.

As Alan regaled her with tales of fairs gone by, Greer found herself getting swept up in his infectious enthusiasm. She could practically taste the exotic street food, hear the pulsing beat of live music, and feel the crackling energy of a community united in celebration. It was the kind of immersive, boundary-pushing experience she craved, both personally and professionally.

But even more tantalizing was the thought of experiencing it all with a new friend by her side. In the short time she'd known Alan, he'd awakened a part of her she'd thought long dormant. The idea of exploring this vibrant new world with him, of forging a genuine connection, filled her with a heady mix of excitement and terror.

Greer knew all too well the perils of letting people get too close. Friendship came with strings, expectations she invariably failed to meet. It was safer to keep things superficial, to hide behind the polished façade of her writing. In her articles, she was in control, free to craft the perfect narrative. Real life was messy, unpredictable, and impossible to revise.

When Alan casually mentioned introducing her

to friends, Greer felt the familiar walls slamming up. "Sounds great," she replied, the words ringing hollow even to her own ears.

Alan cocked an eyebrow, clearly picking up on her sudden reticence.

Greer forced herself to take a breath, to push past the knee-jerk weakness to retreat. "I mean it, I'd love to meet them," she amended, mustering a smile that almost felt genuine.

The prospect of navigating new social waters filled Greer with dread. Small talk, subtle cues, the constant pressure to perform—it was an exhausting dance she'd never quite mastered. But something about Alan's earnest enthusiasm made her want to try, to believe that this time could be different.

Greer tried to wrap her head around the thrilling prospects that lay ahead. With Alan's insider knowledge of the art scene and her instincts for unearthing the extraordinary, they could be an unstoppable duo, poised to take the city by storm. The anticipation sent a shiver down her spine, daring her to step outside her carefully constructed comfort zone. Yet, a nagging voice whispered in the back of her mind—would Alan still stick around once he glimpsed the real Greer, the one she kept hidden behind her polished veneer?

As Greer surveyed her new surroundings, a strange sense of belonging washed over her. After a whirlwind of impersonal hotel rooms and fleeting sublets, the idea of putting down roots felt both alien and exhilarating.

Sinking into the well-worn armchair, Greer marveled at the serendipitous path that had led her to this very moment. Her globe-trotting ways had always baffled her homebody siblings, who couldn't imagine life beyond their familiar haunts. But here, in this vibrant space pulsing with creative energy, Greer knew she'd finally found her element.

Her gaze wandered the room, drinking in the eclectic mix of art and artifacts that whispered tales of lives well-lived. Each piece held a story begging to be unraveled, not unlike the ancient sites she'd explored on her own far-flung adventures. The difference, of course, was that this time she had a guide to bring those stories to life.

Eyes fluttering shut, Greer tuned in to the gentle rhythm of the city outside, a soothing backdrop to the excitement buzzing within her. One thing was crystal clear—life with Alan and Phoenix was going to be anything but boring.

CHAPTER
NINE

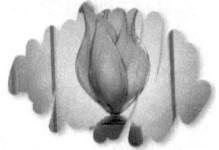

S unlight streamed through the gallery's floor-to-ceiling windows, bathing Greer's laptop in a warm glow as she stared at the unfinished headlines. For hours, she'd been trying to capture the essence of San Francisco's dynamic art scene, a struggle that mirrored her own journey of rediscovering herself. The city's foggy mornings and imaginative spirit called to her, promising change, but a nagging voice in her head wondered if she was still running away.

The cursor blinked on the empty page, taunting her. Three hundred blog posts under her belt, and she couldn't even come up with a decent headline for her first article. Maybe she should stick to writing blog posts about hidden temples in Thailand or secret waterfalls in Costa Rica. In those places, she understood her role—the fearless traveler, always watching but never truly fitting in.

Greer's fingers danced across the keys, her brow furrowed as she tried out another headline idea. The gentle sounds of Alan arranging the gallery and the smooth jazz floating through the air wrapped around her like a comforting blanket, a familiarity she'd grown accustomed to over the past weeks. She breathed in deeply, the combined aromas of fresh flowers and coffee filling her nostrils, and let herself relax into the sense of belonging. A feeling that still scared her more than she wanted to admit.

This place was starting to feel too much like home. But there was something about Alan's authentic kindness and the gallery's peaceful vibe that made her want to stick around, and that frightened her more than any far-flung adventure ever could. She was tucked into a plush chair in a corner of the room, enjoying the vibe of the empty gallery in the early morning.

"Hey Alan, what do you think about 'San Francisco: Where Art Meets Heart'?" Greer asked, glancing over at him as he rearranged a new sculpture display near the window.

Gah, that headline was terrible. She came across like a starry-eyed tourist, not a serious journalist. What a sappy excuse for creativity. She winced at how ridiculous it sounded even to her. *It could be worse; I could be aiming for something as banal as Sourdough and Secrets, or Fog and Blogs: A Midlife Crisis Memoir, or worse, Cats, Corpses, and Cable Cars.* She groaned.

Alan whirled around, a teasing grin on his face that didn't quite reach his eyes. "Sweetie, that's so corny it could be served on the cob. We need something with a bit more... pizzazz!" His hands fidgeted restlessly at his sides, a nervous habit she'd noticed more frequently these days. He fiddled with his rings like a magician about to pull a rabbit out of thin air. Hopefully not a confession.

Greer threw him an overly dramatic eye roll, but couldn't stop herself from smiling. "Coming from the man who says 'darling' like he's auditioning for Gatsby."

Alan looked down his nose at her and preened, as only he could do.

Greer chuckled. "Alright then, Captain Pizzazz. Dazzle me with your brilliant suggestions."

Their playful back-and-forth felt as cozy as her favorite sweater, even while she noted the subtle changes in Alan's behavior. Something wasn't quite right.

"Get ready for this: 'Golden Gate Dreams: San Francisco's Artistic Awakening'!" Alan proclaimed, his hands gesturing grandly, but Greer spotted a faint tremor in his fingers that hadn't been there before.

His fingers fluttered too long near the edge of the canvas. Greer had seen that kind of stall before —when someone needed a moment to lie convincingly.

Her internal radar pinged. He was hiding something. The way his movements felt just a tad too exaggerated, as if he were overcompensating.

She turned the headline over in her mind, tapping her pen against her chin. "You know what? That's actually pretty stinkin' good. Consider it stolen." Greer watched Alan out of the corner of her eye, sensing that his typical flair for the dramatic felt a bit forced today, like a well-worn costume that no longer fit quite right.

As she jotted down the headline, Greer marveled at how effortlessly she'd slipped into this new chapter of her life. The gallery had become her haven, its vibrant energy sparking her creativity in ways she never thought possible. After smothering her wild imagination to appease everyone around her, she finally felt free to breathe again.

Living above the gallery felt right in a way her previous life never had. Here, surrounded by art and authenticity, she could finally shed the polished persona she'd maintained for so long.

Alan sauntered over and plopped down on the arm of her chair, his presence feeling strangely heavy. "I gotta say, having you as a roommate has been a total trip. You're like the level-headed sister I never had, keeping me in check when I get too carried away with my own fabulousness."

Fabulous. She'd always dreamed of being some-one's sensible sibling. Next stop: honorary hall monitor. Her muscles tensed at his closeness, that old instinct to maintain her carefully guarded personal space. Too many so-called friends who'd turned out not to have her best interests at heart… But Alan had somehow become the exception to all her rules.

Greer arched an eyebrow, pushing down the urge to create some distance between them. "Can't tell if that's a compliment or a subtle dig, but I'll take it. Though since I do have sisters, trust me when I say you're better off as an only child."

The words came out lighter than she felt.

Beneath her quip lurked the familiar fear of attachment, of allowing someone close enough to matter. Her independence had always been her armor.

"Oh, don't be ridiculous!" Alan scoffed, clutching his chest in mock indignation, but Greer caught a flicker of vulnerability beneath his bravado. "It's the ultimate compliment, darling. Who else could keep me grounded while I'm off being my marvelous self?"

They both burst into laughter, the familiar banter chipping away at the walls. It still caught her off guard how effortlessly Alan had managed to slip past her defenses, his infectious energy impossible to resist.

Greer's instincts nagged at her, refusing to ignore the oddities she'd noticed around the gallery recently. Right now, her gut reminded her that this tranquil artistic haven concealed shadowy secrets. She caught Alan's reflection in an antique mirror as he fidgeted with a sculpture by the window, his hands trembling ever so slightly. Alan was an amazing friend. He was her flamboyant, big-hearted roommate. A man she was sure could be old enough to be her father, the man who'd offered her a home when she needed it most. He had avoided talking about the night in the alley.

Her stomach knotted, recognizing the signs of someone grappling with a secret they couldn't share.

"Alan?" Greer's voice cut through the air as she snapped her laptop shut. "What are you hiding from me?" The question hung between them, a ticking time bomb. She'd mastered that tone during countless arguments with her evasive ex. Direct, demanding, yet laced with just enough concern to keep them talking.

Alan's phone buzzed, shattering the tense silence. The color drained from his face as he checked the screen, his carefully crafted facade cracking for a fleeting instant.

"Excuse me, darling. I need to take this." He vanished into his office, but not before Greer glimpsed the caller ID: "Detective K.B."

Her mind shifted into high gear, cataloging every detail, every nuance. The nervous clink of Alan's rings, the slight hitch in his voice, the hurried shuffle of his designer loafers across the hardwood. Feigning focus on her work, Greer strained to over-hear Alan's muffled conversation. After a week of living above the gallery, she'd discovered the walls concealed more than just art. The snippets she caught made her pulse race. "...it's not what you're thinking,   Kyle..."   and   "...Grandfather's collection..."

As night descended, Greer climbed the stairs to their shared apartment, her thoughts entangled in the enigmas surrounding the gallery. She should let it go, concentrate on her looming deadline, and quit playing amateur sleuth. But the relentless curiosity that had propelled her here wouldn't allow her to rest.

CHAPTER

TEN

A lan walked away to finish his conversation, and Greer bent her head back to focus on her laptop. The time whittled away as she became immersed in work. Her worldview narrowing to only the words flowing from her fingertips.

The gallery hummed with quiet energy—staff adjusting lights, measuring distances. Sunlight spilled across the hardwood, catching on frames Alan had leaned in neat rows.

Greer sat curled in a lounge chair, Phoenix crammed into the small space behind her laptop as his tail thumped across her lap. She stroked his fur absently, content to watch the careful choreography unfold.

Alan crossed the room, sharp eyes scanning a canvas. "I think this one anchors the room," he said, then looked at her, a smile tugging. "By the way, have you decided what you'll wear?"

Her hand stilled. "What I'll wear?"

"For the opening," he clarified, as if it were obvious. "You're planning to attend, right?"

Heat prickled her cheeks. She shifted in her seat, stalling. "I didn't... I wasn't sure I was expected to."

Alan blinked, clearly blindsided. "Not expected?" His voice rose in disbelief, though not unkindly. "Of course you are. You're part of this place now. Why would you imagine otherwise?"

A hollow laugh slipped from her throat. "I guess I just didn't think... well, I don't exactly have anything to wear."

Something softened in his eyes. "No formal clothes? Surely you packed at least a few things."

"When I left Denver, I left that world behind. Galas, heels, cocktail dresses—sold or donated."

"This isn't a gala. But it is important." Alan's expression softened, but a glint remained. "The biggest opening in two years," he continued. "Press, collectors, critics. I want you there—not in borrowed clothes, but as yourself. Present. Confident."

"I don't even own heels anymore," she said, half-laughing.

"That won't do." He nodded toward the street. "There's a vintage boutique two doors down. It's full of pieces with character—designer, but not suffocating."

Greer stiffened. "Alan, that sounds… expensive."

He waved it off. "Fabulous doesn't mean new. It means a story."

"I just don't want to disappoint you," she mumbled.

He stepped closer. "Think of the investigation… Everyone you should meet will be there."

She rolled her eyes, but her laugh was genuine this time. "Fine. But if I end up in sequins, I'm blaming you."

Alan straightened, a mock salute in her direction. "Deal. No sequins. Just stunning."

She let out a breath and shook her head, though hesitation still tugged at the edges. Greer was still shaking her head when Alan suddenly clapped his hands together, mischief sparking in his eyes. "It's decided then."

"Decided?" she echoed warily.

"You," he declared in a deliberately over-the-top drawl, his voice dipping into mock sophistication, "are going to look spectacular." He accompanied it with an extravagant sweep of his hands—more stage flourish than real drama—but the twinkle in his gaze betrayed his amusement. Only a man utterly at ease in his skin could have pulled it off without self-consciousness.

Greer couldn't help it; she laughed. "Oh no…"

"Oh yes." Alan leaned forward and, with one fingertip, gently pressed the top of her open laptop until it clicked shut. Before she could protest, he extended his hand. "Let's go."

Her eyes widened. "Now?"

"Always." He slid her hand into his, tugging her lightly from the chair and then tucking her arm neatly into the crook of his elbow.

"Alan—" she began, but his stride had already carried them halfway across the gallery floor, Phoenix winding around their ankles like a furry chaperone.

"Marco! Back in a couple of hours—hold the fort!"

From the ladder, Marco saluted without looking down.

Alan swept her through the doors before she could regroup. The gallery noise faded. Cool salt air kissed her cheeks.

She glanced up at him, bemused. "You don't let people argue, do you?"

"That's the trick," he said, guiding her like it was second nature. "No second thoughts. Just trust me."

———

ALAN PUSHED OPEN THE GLASS-PANED DOOR AND ushered her inside, his arm still looped through hers. A bell jingled overhead, and the air shifted, warm with the faint perfume of cedar and old fabric. The boutique gleamed—a jewel box of silks, satins, and beadwork. Every piece whispered of another era.

"Carla!" Alan's voice rolled out, rich with delight.

From behind a counter stacked with hatboxes, a woman in her sixties emerged, sharp in a wide-legged pantsuit and horn-rimmed glasses. "Alan Caputo, as I live and breathe. And who's this?"

"This is Greer Caldwell," he said with a flourish. "She's going to Rivera's opening and needs something that says effortless magnificence."

Carla's eyes sparkled. "Ah. A canvas."

Greer flushed. "More like a mannequin," she muttered, but they were already off.

Alan was already rifling through a rack. "No sequins. No feathers. Nothing from a cotillion. We want timeless. Playful. Striking."

Carla laughed, already moving toward a rack of muted jewel tones. "So nothing dramatic then."

"I'm standing right here," Greer mumbled.

Carla winked. "Every woman needs an advocate. He's a good one."

She turned to Alan. "I'm so glad you are back and better than ever. You had me worried there for a minute, my friend."

"Does that kind of thing happen around here often?" Greer asked.

"No, not at all. We are a small, tight-knit community here in the district. We all watch out for each other. That's the way it's always been. I have to believe this is just the Tenderloin spilling over, like it does every once in a while."

"Exactly," Alan said with a chuckle, changing the uncomfortable topic.

Greer let it drop. She wouldn't learn anything here.

"Anyway. She has taste," Alan said, "but she's hiding behind loafers and button-downs."

"Elegance with ease," Carla agreed. "Something that whispers."

"Exactly," Alan said. "Think Lanvin. Vionnet. Presence without pretense."

Carla held up an olive sheath. "Clean lines. Square neck."

Alan shook his head. "Corporate gala."

"Agreed." She hung it back.

A champagne wrap dress followed. Alan pressed a hand to his chest. "Closer, but… whispering too softly."

Greer muttered, "Whispering sounds fine."

They ignored her.

Next: a scarlet column.

Alan shook his head. "She'll vanish into Rivera's palette—and complain she can't sit."

Carla didn't flinch. "Noted. We want impact, not intimidation."

Then: a midnight-blue jumpsuit—wide-legged, tailored, neckline plunging but elegant.

Alan exhaled. "Yes. Yes. YES."

Carla smiled. "This one has presence."

Greer raised a brow. "A jumpsuit? Isn't that... casual?"

Alan scoffed. "Darling, this is a power move. Belt it right, add earrings, and the room will hush."

Carla handed it over. "Try it on."

Greer swallowed hard, staring at the pantsuit as if it might vanish. She accepted the hanger gingerly, fingers tightening on the silk, and for the first time, she felt a flicker of curiosity, not dread, about what she might see in the mirror. She wasn't this woman anymore. Or so she thought—until Alan's hand steadied her.

"Greer," he said gently. "This is you."

Reluctantly, Greer took it and slipped behind the dressing curtain. The fabric slid over her body with surprising ease, the wide legs swishing softly as she turned in the mirror. She stepped out, tugging self-consciously at the waist.

Alan pressed a hand to his chest, his grin irrepressible. "Mahvelous, dahling. Absolutely mahvelous." He twirled his hand in a flamboyant little circle. "That neckline! That drape! You're a goddess, and you don't even know it."

Carla nodded in approval. "That's the one. She doesn't have to shout. She'll walk into the room, and people will lean forward to listen."

Her throat tightened, but the smile came anyway. "It's… more than I planned to spend."

Alan waved a dismissive hand. "An investment."

Carla chuckled. "Every woman deserves one piece that makes her feel invincible. Now, let's accessorize to finish this off right."

Alan made a dramatic "chef's kiss" motion. "Now we're cooking."

Carla wasn't finished. From a tray she drew out earrings—drops of rock crystal, clear as water, set in delicate filigree silver. They sparkled, but softly, like moonlight rather than spotlight.

Greer hesitated. "I usually just wear studs."

Alan plucked them from Carla's hand. "These aren't earrings. They're punctuation."

He fastened them gently. The crystals brushed her jaw.

Greer's lips parted. "Oh."

"See?" Carla said. "Just right."

"Shoes!" Alan declared, crouching like a sommelier. He held up black satin mules. "Elegant. Timeless. Comfy."

Greer eyed them warily. "They look… tall."

"Three inches," Alan countered. "Darling, that's practically a sneaker."

Greer rolled her eyes but couldn't smother a laugh.

"Wait," Carla murmured. She returned with a black satin clutch, beaded in Art Deco swirls.

Alan sucked in his breath. "Carla, you genius."

Carla placed it gently into Greer's hands. "It's the perfect scale for the jumpsuit. Just enough detail to remind people you have style, without stealing the show."

Greer turned it over in her palms. The beading shimmered faintly under the lights, understated but confident. She pressed her lips together, caught between disbelief and a strange, growing pleasure.

Alan studied her like a curator spotting a masterpiece. "You walked in here Denver, but you're leaving San Francisco."

Carla smiled. "Not someone new. Just more you."

Greer studied the mirror. Jumpsuit. Belt. Earrings. Clutch. Not gaudy. Not excessive. Just... her. She exhaled. "It's beautiful."

Alan grinned, triumphant. "Darling, it's more than beautiful. It's you."

Greer's head bobbed once in response as she silently slipped back into the dressing room to return to her comfort clothes.

Once she returned to the main room, Carla whisked the pieces into careful tissue and a garment bag, tying the package with satin ribbon.

Alan handed over his card before Greer could reach for hers. She protested, "Alan, no—"

Carla interrupted smoothly with a waved hand. "It's settled. The outfit chose you. Logistics are boring."

Greer bit back a smile as Alan guided her toward the door, garment bag swinging between them.

Outside, the late afternoon sun lit the sidewalk. Alan gave a contented sigh. "Like I said before. Mahvelous, dahling. Absolutely mahvelous." He twirled his hand in mock flourish again.

Greer shook her head, half-exasperated, half-amused. "What have I gotten myself into?"

Alan looped her arm through his once more. "Into fun, darling. Into joy. Into being exactly who you are, without apology."

And for the first time, Greer thought maybe— just maybe—he was right.

ELEVEN

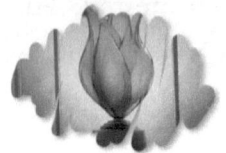

Nestled in the cozy window seat, Greer clutched her notebook, a bittersweet cocktail of contentment and unease swirling within her. Just like every other time, she'd gotten too comfortable somewhere. The second she let her guard down, everything went pear-shaped. This vibrant, artistic sanctuary was a far cry from the sterile minimalism her ex-husband had insisted upon, yet it felt inexplicably right. She'd come to San Francisco seeking a fresh start, and amidst the whirlwind of art and camaraderie, she'd found it—even as a part of her braced for the inevitable storm.

"Greer, darling!" Alan's singsong voice drifted from the kitchen, jolting her from her reverie. "I've just popped open a positively sinful Barolo. Care to indulge with me?"

Despite his airy tone, Greer detected a slight tremor, a dead giveaway that something was eating at him.

A gentle smile tugging at her lips, Greer glanced at her notebook, her fingers grazing the well-worn pages. The familiar feel of the paper anchored her, each page brimming with musings that may never see the light of day in her articles. Intimate reflections that revealed more about herself than any destination ever could. Setting it down on the table beside her, she called out, "On my way!" Unwinding her legs, she left the comfort of the oversized leather chair, heading in his direction, her bare feet gliding across the cool hardwood, each step a tangible reminder that this place had become her safe haven.

In the kitchen, Alan poured two generous glasses of wine, his hands steady but his shoulders coiled with tension. The room practically crackled with unspoken words. As he turned to face her, his signature grin seemed forced.

"I thought we earned a little indulgence after that creative heavy lifting," he quipped, pressing a glass into her hand. The wine's rich, dark fruit notes intertwined with whispers of earth and spice.

They melted into the plush sofa, Alan draping himself across one end with his usual theatrical panache, but Greer couldn't help but zero in on the restless tapping of his fingers against the polished leather. Her analytical mind kicked into overdrive, documenting every detail as if she were crafting another blog. The tightness in his shoulders, that strained smile, the atypical quiet. Whatever was troubling him would come out sooner or later. She had already experienced in their short time knowing each other that Alan could never keep a secret for long. A soothing warmth pressed against her thigh, and she glanced down to find Phoenix curled up beside her, his fiery orange fur a vivid contrast to the deep chocolate beneath him.

"Well, hello there, handsome," Greer cooed, her fingers finding that sweet spot behind Phoenix's ears that made him melt into a puddle of purrs. The cat's contented kneading against her thigh grounded her, a soothing rhythm amidst the unspoken tension in the room.

Alan leaned over, his hand joining Greer's in the feline lovefest. "Looks like our little prince has claimed another loyal subject, eh?" His eyes did not quite match the mirth in his voice. Greer's senses tingled, recognizing the signs of an emotional struggle, but she knew better than to push. Timing was everything when it came to unraveling secrets.

A chuckle escaped her lips as she marveled at how these two had managed to wriggle past her carefully constructed walls. The intrepid journalist, outsmarted by a charming cat and an equally beguiling roommate. "Pretty sure he's got us both wrapped around his furry little paw. Bet he understands every word we say, the sneaky devil."

As if on cue, Phoenix chirped and headbutted Alan's hand, shamelessly demanding more attention.

"And there's the proof," Greer snickered, amused by the cat's antics. "Clever boy knows exactly how to get what he wants."

Alan's fingers absently traced the rim of his wineglass, his gaze distant, pensive. The question that had been niggling at Greer for weeks now bubbled to the surface, a missing piece in the puzzle of her friend's life.

Unable to contain her curiosity any longer, Greer took the plunge. "So, Alan, I've been wondering… Tell me more about your family and the Bayside Art Collective? How'd you end up with it if that wasn't your dream?"

In one swift motion, Alan downed half his wine, launching into the story with his usual flair, but Greer couldn't ignore the faint tremor in his usually steady hands. "Oh, honey, it's quite the wild ride. Buckle up!"

Alan's signature poise seemed to falter, his manicured nails tapping an anxious rhythm against the delicate stemware. Greer's journalistic instincts hummed with suspicion. There was more to this tale than met the eye, and she had a feeling the real story would be far juicier than the polished version Alan was about to spin.

"Gramps was a real maverick, you know," Alan began, his wine sloshing dangerously close to the rim as he gesticulated.

She resisted the urge to pull out her notebook. The way Alan clutched his wineglass, the way he glanced at the darkened hallway—it all felt rehearsed. Like a story he'd told a dozen times, each version polished a little smoother.

"He didn't start with the gallery, though. Never one for stocks or any of that Wall Street bullshit. Art was his game, and he played it like a pro." His voice caught slightly, a flicker of emotion betraying his nonchalant facade. "When the market tanked in '29, he was one of the few still standing tall. People were desperate, those here who had lost everything, those fleeing Europe and selling off their treasures to escape. Gramps stepped up, offering them a chance to protect what little they could, while helping them, and promising to keep their pieces safe until they could afford to buy 'em back."

Greer's historian side recoiled at the unspoken implications. She'd heard countless tales of lost and looted art, the heavy silence between the lines speaking volumes. Her instinct was to press for more, to scribble furiously in her notebook, but she reined it in. This was Alan, baring his soul, not just another story.

The wine turned bitter on her tongue, the rich notes souring with each revelation.

"Some of these pieces? Absolute masterpieces, Greer. Real heavy-hitters." Alan's grip tightened on his glass, his knuckles white. "At first, Gramps opened the gallery to keep the art safe, let people see it for a small fee. Like his own little museum, you know?"

She managed a nod, her throat constricting with dawning comprehension.

"When spit hit the fan in Europe, Gramps made

it his mission to help families get out," Alan confided, his bravado crumbling. "They trusted him with their collections, praying he'd keep it all safe 'til they could come back." His eyes shimmered, the weight of generations pressing down on him.

Greer's fingers trembled against the delicate stemware, the gravity of Alan's revelation hitting her like a sucker punch to the gut. The historian in her yearned to unravel every thread of this tangled web, to expose the dark underbelly of the art world. But the friend in her? She just wanted to wrap Alan in a bear hug and shield him from the heartbreak that was sure to come.

"Goodness gracious, Alan," she murmured. "That's heavy stuff. I can't even imagine the burden you've been carrying all these years."

Alan nodded, his shoulders sagging under the weight of his family's legacy. "It's been eating away at me, Greer. I mean, how the heck do I make this right? These paintings, these sculptures—they're not just objects. They're pieces of people's lives, their histories."

He leaned forward, his elbows resting on his knees, his gaze fixed on the antique rug beneath their feet. "My grandfather, followed by my father, spent years tracking down the original owners, or at least their descendants. Which is why most of them have never been sold. They've hung on the walls here at home, or in the Gallery as part of a show only. But it's like searching for a needle in a bloomin' haystack, and with the gallery struggling, it was all too much."

Greer's heart clenched, the little things she'd noticed but brushed off. The hushed phone calls, the late-night meetings, the way Alan clammed up whenever she asked about certain pieces. It all made sense now.

"You've been selling them off, haven't you?" she asked gently, her hand finding his, giving it a reassuring squeeze. "To keep the gallery afloat?"

Alan's head snapped up, his eyes wide with panic. "I swear it's not like that. My grandfather hired a law firm. They were working with various organizations like the Commission for Looted Art in Europe, the Art Loss Register, and Lost Art Database run by the German Lost Art Foundation. Even the Jewish Digital Cultural Recovery Project. I'm sure there are others the lawyers work with; those are just off the top of my head. When they figured there were no descendants or heirs, or those found were unable or uninterested in repurchasing the art, rather than risk these works vanishing into private hands, our family decided to sell them—selectively and carefully—to public institutions committed to ethical curation and historical transparency. Each museum that received a piece agreed to preserve the full provenance, including the name of the original owner, and to display it as part of the broader human story it represents. In this way, we hoped these works continued to honor the lives they once touched and stand as a testament to survival, dignity, and remembrance."

Greer bobbed her head in understanding.

"I don't know why the gallery is in the red. Nothing's changed in years. My overhead is small, and I don't have any crazy spending habits. I've considered selling, of course, but while their provenance is solid, the records impeccable, it's still such a morally gray area. I've struggled with the burden of it all… Anyway, it's less about any sale and more about the lawyer fees that I can't afford right now."

Her thoughts spun, her journalist's instincts kicking into high gear. This was the story of a lifetime, a case of a family of heroes trying to save history, or a scandal in the making if twisted just right, that could rock the art world to its core. If the case of the 'Woman in Gold' was anything to go by.

But this was her friend. She couldn't just hang him out to dry.

"We'll figure this out, Alan," she said firmly, her voice steady despite the adrenaline coursing through her veins.

Suddenly, a blood-curdling yowl pierced the air, sending shivers down Greer's spine. Phoenix stood rigid in the doorway, his hackles raised, his eyes fixed on something outside the window. Greer whipped around just in time to catch a shadowy figure darting past, a blur of movement that shouldn't have been possible two stories up.

"What the…" she hissed, her heart hammering against her ribs. "Did you see that?"

Alan was on his feet in an instant, his wine glass forgotten on the coffee table. "I saw it," he confirmed, his voice tight with tension. "But how? There's no fire escape on that side of the building."

Fragments of logic warring with the impossible scene she'd just witnessed bounced around her head. No ledge, no handholds, nothing but smooth brick and glass. Yet, someone had been there, watching them, listening.

She reached for Alan's hand, her fingers intertwining with his, anchoring them both in the midst of the chaos. "We're in this together, okay?" she murmured, her voice soft but fierce. "You, me, and Phoenix. We'll get to the bottom of this, I promise."

Alan's eyes met hers, a flicker of hope amidst the fear and uncertainty. "I'm really glad you're here, Greer," he said, his voice raw with emotion. "I don't know what I'd do without you."

Reaching for Alan's quivering hand, Greer gave him a gentle squeeze. "Hey," she said softly, a tender smile tugging at her lips. "There's nowhere else I'd rather be." The words seemed inadequate, but she hoped they conveyed the depth of her feelings.

How did she explain that this messy, brilliant chaos was the only place that didn't make her want to run?

Alan's hand tightened around hers, his rings a comforting pressure against her skin. "I know, darling. I know." His voice cracked, a rare glimpse of vulnerability peeking through his usually unflappable exterior. Greer's stomach dropped, but she let the moment pass without comment.

TWELVE

T he garment bag had hung on the back of her closet door all week, a quiet sentinel watching her every morning and evening. At first, it made her uneasy. Thoughts of its contents mocked her. Too fancy, too deliberate, too much like the old Greer who lived in other people's expectations. But over the days, the unease softened. She stopped averting her eyes. She even found herself reaching inside and brushing her fingers over the draped crepe once or twice, feeling the fabric's cool promise beneath her touch.

Now it was the moment of truth.

She stood barefoot in her little sanctuary within Alan's apartment above the gallery, Phoenix curled in his usual patch of sunlight on the bed. The garment bag lay open, the jumpsuit waiting.

Greer exhaled and stepped into it. The fabric slid over her skin, whisper-smooth. She zipped it up, cinched the gold-clasped belt at her waist, and slipped on the suede mules. She clipped in the crystal earrings and picked up the beaded clutch.

And then she turned to the mirror.

For a long, startled moment, she simply stared.

The reflection wasn't the Denver socialite she'd tried to be—polished to a sheen, armored in gowns meant to impress donors. Nor was it the newly divorced woman who'd shown up in San Francisco with little more than a suitcase and a stray cat as company.

This woman was… something in between. Stronger. Quieter. Her collarbones glowed under the bateau neckline, the belt drew her figure into clean, confident lines, and the crystals at her ears caught the light each time she moved. It wasn't a costume. It wasn't a disguise. It was her.

Phoenix stretched, leapt to the floor, and padded over to rub against her ankle. She bent, stroking his fur, whispering, "Well? What do you think?"

He purred in approval.

Greer smiled faintly. "Okay then. Guess it's show time."

With a sigh, she made her way down the stairs.

ALAN WAS ALREADY IN THE GALLERY, A WHIRL OF energy as final lighting checks and catering trays bustled around him. The room shimmered under track lights angled toward Rivera's canvases, jewel-toned storms of paint that seemed to pulse with life. Guests would be arriving within the hour.

Greer hovered at the back door, suddenly unsure. She felt… exposed.

Alan looked up, caught sight of her, and froze mid-gesture. His hands pressed to his chest. "Stop. Everyone stop. Look at her!"

Marco, adjusting a frame, blinked upward. The catering staff paused, confused.

Greer flushed scarlet. "Alan, don't—"

Alan ignored her entirely, striding across the gallery to meet her at the bottom step. He offered his arm with a theatrical flourish, his grin incandescent. "Darling. You are breathtaking."

Alan guided her to the long gilt mirror that hung near his office, a piece of gallery décor more decorative than functional. He positioned her before it with ceremony.

"Now," he said softly, his flamboyance fading for a heartbeat, but the sparkle in his eyes warming into sincerity. "See what I see."

Greer stared at her reflection—stronger, steadier, more herself than she'd dared imagine.

Not just the jumpsuit, not just the belt and earrings and clutch. She saw a woman who belonged here—not as an interloper, not as a mannequin, but as herself.

Her throat tightened. "Alan…"

He squeezed her arm gently. "You don't need to thank me, Greer. You did this."

Greer flushed scarlet under his theatrical praise. "You're impossible," she muttered, half-exasperated, half-amused.

Alan's grin only widened. At that moment, a cork popped across the gallery, followed by another, the sound echoing like applause. He lifted his hand, sprinkling invisible glitter into the air with a flourish.

"Impossible?" he echoed, eyes dancing. "Darling, the only difference between impossible and I'm possible is a little sparkle and a breath of space." He swooshed his hand as if scattering stardust. "And poof—look at you. You're possible. Always."

Greer laughed, the tightness in her chest loosening. He had her back—ridiculous gestures, glitter, and all. Trust Alan to turn her protest into a mantra —and somehow make her believe it.

Phoenix, having followed her downstairs like a furry usher, twined around her ankles and let out a timely meow, as if to seal the moment.

Alan laughed, tension breaking. "See? Even Phoenix approves."

THE DOOR CHIMED. THE FIRST WAVE OF GUESTS swept in—critics, collectors, friends of Rivera. Conversation lifted like champagne bubbles, laughter and exclamations filling the gallery space.

Greer's pulse leapt. Never comfortable being at the center of things. But Alan's steady presence at her side, his earlier words echoing—*You're possible. Always*—anchored her.

She caught her reflection one last time in the gilt mirror before turning to greet the crowd. The woman staring back looked ready.

And Greer believed she just might be.

Alan squeezed her hand as they paused between

conversations. "Trust your instincts. Tonight, it begins," he murmured, eyes flicking toward the crowd.

Greer swallowed hard. She wasn't an investigator. She was a writer who noticed details. But maybe that was enough.

Alan squeezed her hand, voice low as he steered her toward the center of the room. "You'll do fabulously, darling. Just keep noticing."

Greer swallowed hard. *Noticing* was all she had. And tonight, it had to be enough.

Marco intercepted them first, sleeves rolled back, a glass in one hand and a tray of programs in the other. His perpetual air of competence hadn't slipped even under the crush of guests.

"Everything's running smoothly," he assured Alan, his voice calm, his gaze sweeping the room like a quiet conductor. "Rivera's pleased, the critics are already taking notes.

Alan beamed. "Marco, you really are my left and right hand, my sanity and my ulcer, all rolled into one. Truly, the gallery would fall into the Bay without you."

"Lighting's perfect," he murmured to Alan, then to Greer, with a wink, "And so are you." He evaporated before she could laugh—reappearing near the bar to charm a critic, then at the far wall explaining Rivera's underpainting to a woman with a set of tasteful pearls. She was struck again by how comfortable he seemed in this world. He moved through the crowd as though he belonged to everyone and no one—trading a word here, a laugh there, always present at the edges of her vision.

Greer felt like she was in a fishbowl. Quite a few people caught her eye and gave her a perfunctory nod, while a couple of people openly stared at her. It was unnerving.

Then the temperature shifted by a fraction. The crowd thinned as if making way for weather. Across the room, a man hovered on the edge of conversations, never quite at the center but never absent. Tall, dark suit, posture composed—he gave the impression of a man who absorbed everything while saying little, but somehow his presence carried weight. Greer noted the way his gaze flicked from her to the crowd, as though measuring the whole room with quiet calculation. People seemed to give him space without ever acknowledging that they had.

He moved through the crowd like a shadow sliding across a wall, and then suddenly he was there, directly in their path, offering no chance to sidestep.

"Alan," he said, extending a hand. "Congratulations on the show. It's been a while." Polished, professional, nothing extra.

Alan's smile met the room's requirements. "Dominic. Good to see you." His jaw ticked once, so faint she wouldn't have seen it if she hadn't been staring. Dominic's gaze found Greer.

Alan coughed. "Meet Greer—she sees what others miss."

The statement flowed easily, but there was an unusual stiffness in his voice. The words struck her, though Alan likely meant them as harmless flair. Dominic's smile was faint, almost polite, his handshake firm but brief.

"Welcome," he said, the single word clipped, deliberate. His eyes lingered on her a beat too long before sliding away.

Greer murmured a polite reply, but Alan's fingers pressed lightly at her elbow. Still smiling for Dominic's benefit, he gave her a quick sidelong glance—an almost imperceptible '*later*'.

It was like Alan was shielding her from something invisible, as though Dominic carried a contagion only he recognized. Protective, the way a person stands between you and a street you haven't noticed is busy.

Greer filed it away, feeling the tension hum beneath the surface of the crowd's polite laughter.

The exchange lasted only moments before Dominic melted back into the crowd, but the air felt different in his wake. It wasn't hostility, exactly, but something Alan clearly wasn't ready to discuss in public.

THE GALLERY DOOR CHIMED AGAIN, MORE LAUGHTER and coats rustling as Rivera's circle swept inside. Alan greeted them with a host's flourish, his voice rising above the swell. Yet even in motion, he stayed tethered to Greer, a hand at her elbow, a glance tossed her way as if to say, *'You're not alone here.'*

When the new arrivals were safely engaged by Marco, Alan leaned toward her. The sparkle in his expression softened, the showman slipping into something quieter. "Greer," he murmured, "you've no idea what a gift it is—having you here."

Greer blinked, caught off guard. "Me? I've barely been here a month. I'm not—"

"You are," he cut in gently. "Phoenix keeps the gallery from feeling hollow. And you—" his hand fluttered, as if no words quite captured it, "you've kept *me* from feeling hollow."

Her breath caught.

The words weren't romantic. They didn't need to be. It was simpler, deeper—a recognition that somewhere between finding him unconscious in an alley and standing together in silk and starlight, they'd become each other's ballast.

Greer leaned down and smoothed a hand over Phoenix's back as the cat twined between them. "I'm still finding my feet," she admitted, voice low. "New city. New life. Some days it feels like I'm pretending I belong."

Alan's gaze warmed, steady. "Pretending? Darling, look around you. You've already woven yourself in. Guests will forget half the paintings by morning, but they'll remember you. Because you're real."

Something eased inside her, the way tension unspools after being held too long.

A fresh burst of laughter rolled from across the room. Alan glanced up, squared his shoulders, and slipped the host's mask back on. But as he moved to greet another guest, his hand brushed hers in passing—a silent *I've got you.*

Greer stood a little taller. Phoenix settled at her

feet, a mascot for them both. And just like that, she felt less like an outsider and more like someone who had roots beginning to take hold.

A WOMAN APPROACHED, IMPOSSIBLE TO OVERLOOK—draped in ivory silk, posture so perfect it made Greer want to stand taller. Every gesture precise. Every line of her face gleamed with polish, but the cool appraisal in her eyes was unmistakable. She glided through the room like a queen surveying territory she already claimed.

Alan's smile was genuine when he greeted her. "Vivian, luminous as ever. You make the walls jealous."

Vivian's lips curved politely, though warmth never reached her gaze. "Alan, you've outdone yourself. A bold choice for Rivera's centerpiece—it nearly rivals the Paris showing." Her tone was warm on the surface, but something in the cadence made the words land just shy of generous.

She extended a hand to Greer, manicured fingers cool to the touch, like the tip of an iceberg gleaming under moonlight.

"And you must be the new roommate I've heard about. Alan always had an eye for interesting...

company." The pause was polite, the smile flawless, yet Greer felt the faint sting beneath it—admiration wrapped in condescension.

Greer bobbed her head, suppressing the urge to shiver, already knowing this was a woman who did not melt for anyone.

Alan, oblivious or unwilling to notice, laughed easily. "You'll have to forgive Ms. Sinclair—she's a perfectionist, which is why her gallery shines like a cathedral."

Vivian inclined her head, as though accepting the compliment as her due. "In this world, Alan, there's no second place. But tonight—" her gaze swept the crowded room, pausing a beat on Greer before returning to Alan "—you've made quite a showing."

She drifted away with the same elegant composure, leaving behind the echo of praise that didn't quite feel like praise at all.

THE GALLERY HAD A PARTICULAR SOUND ON NIGHTS like this, Greer decided—like glass singing. Not just the clink of flutes and the soft chime of bracelets, but the way voices struck the white walls and came back bright. Track lights skimmed along Rivera's canvases until the pigments seemed to vibrate: anemone reds, fathomless indigos, a seam of acid yellow veining a storm of cobalt. The air carried cedar from the frames, lemon oil from the floors, and the crisp citrus of champagne.

Alan moved through it all with that unteachable grace of a host who loves his guests. He kept Greer tucked at his elbow the way a conductor keeps a baton in hand—essential, perfectly placed, a pulse he returned to between flourishes. Twice, someone reached for him. Twice, he angled so Greer was included. He wanted her seen, she realized, not as an accessory but as part of the room's design.

A guest brushed Greer's arm. "Your jumpsuit," the woman breathed, with a conspiratorial smile. "That neckline. Divine." Another guest leaned in to praise Alan's curation, then, with equal fervor, the canapés. "Who is responsible for those little blinis? I've already proposed marriage." Greer smiled, thanked, drifted; she was learning how to accept compliments like passing hors d'oeuvres— graciously, and without clinging to anyone.

"So this is the elusive Greer." A man chuckled, as though sharing a joke only he understood. "Alan keeps his treasures hidden far too well. You'll liven things up, I can tell." His smile had a sheen that did not quite reach the eyes.

Alan, oblivious or ignoring the undertone, clapped him on the back. "Greer, this is Xavier Delacroix."

Xavier extended his hand, and Greer accepted it. If Vivian was glacial, Xavier was slick oil. His handshake lingered just a second too long, his cologne sharp enough to sting. He leaned in closer than necessary, flashing a grin too wide.

Greer forced a polite laugh, her instincts recoiling. His tone reeked of sales pitch—ambulance chaser in a designer tie. She could practically see him circling clients like prey.

Before Greer found her words, he'd already turned that exaggerated warmth back on Alan, praising the crowd, the press turnout, the "brilliant audacity" of putting the graphite-cut canvas where the first wave of guests would see it. He had a sales-man's patter, unbroken by breath.

Alan, the smile never left his lips as he nodded to Xavier. "Excuse us, I need to check in with our artist. Be sure to enjoy yourself tonight."

Without a look back, Alan steered Greer away towards Rivera's small group on the other side of the room, almost as if he was putting as much distance between them as possible.

A FRESH WAVE OF GUESTS SPILLED THROUGH THE door; coats vanished; diamonds arrived. Alan was lifted and carried on a current of names and hands. He introduced Greer to a pair of collectors who said "investment" the way some people said "marriage." One of them squeezed her arm. "That belt —subtle, perfect. You look like the room had you in mind." Another guest asked about their erstwhile feline. As if summoned, the cat materialized from nowhere, trotted through a forest of expensive shoes, paused to receive praise as his due, and vanished toward the catering kitchen.

Greer looked up to find the kitchen door closing, soft as a secret. She looked for Marco out of habit. Not at the entrance. Not by the bar. Not near Rivera. Not leaning on any wall. Absence makes its own shape. She didn't feel alarm—just a wobble where a pillar had been. Before the wobble could become a thought, Alan's hand pressed lightly on her back and steered her toward another cluster.

THIRTEEN

Rivera himself drew them like a tide. He still had paint lodged in the cuticles of his nails, which Greer loved him for. "The trick," he said, gesturing at a canvas where a storm-blue field was slashed by a barely-there graphite line, "is knowing when the conversation is over. Paint speaks. You interrupt it long enough, and it stops answering." His hands moved as if he were still drawing in the air.

Her notebook lived in her head, unclipping like muscle memory. Suddenly, there was a sharp clap. Just a brief sharpness that interrupted the chatter. The room grew quiet, voices lowered to a murmur. Alan's voice boomed a welcome before it softened into admiration only art could coax as he introduced Rivera.

Applause popped like corn as Rivera took the floor for a toast. Alan was directly at his side. "To the city," he said, raising his flute, "because it argues with you and makes you better. To galleries that turn argument into conversation. To friends." The last word swelled the room. Alan's eyes were glassy; he kissed the air toward the ceiling, as if the building itself had aided and abetted. Greer clinked a stranger's glass and heard her own laugh come back to her, stronger.

The night swept forward—applause, glasses clinking, after Rivera's short toast, Greer stood with Alan at the heart of it all, surrounded by art, suspects, friends, rivals, and the indefinable hum of a night that felt like it was only just beginning.

She excused herself at last and slipped into the tiny wedge of peace near the street windows. Outside, the city was a looser, louder gallery: headlights, steam rising from a manhole, someone laughing three doors down. Inside, the glass sang. She studied the reflection—her own silhouette superimposed over a Rivera storm—and thought, *I can do this. Not as a detective. As a listener.* People told you what they were, if you let them.

So many people mingled, the crowd gathered and dispersed in waves of sparkling jewels and hints of expensive perfumes.

Greer let herself be nudged toward a canvas that seemed to breathe—midnight blue, a sudden flare of vermilion, the delicacy of three pencil marks that might be birds. She stood close enough to see the brushstrokes unweave. Close enough to smell linseed ghosted from a week ago. Behind her, laughter lifted, then flattened. When she stepped back, they lifted from meaning and became flight. She thought of Denver—how a pen stroke had rewritten her life. How Alan's fingertip had pressed her laptop closed as if to say, *enough.* How impossible had surrendered to I'm possible with one breath and a little space.

Someone bumped her shoulder and apologized. "Forgive me. I was chasing a rumor that Alan bribed the lights," the man grinned. "I told him he could have my lunch money if he'd tell me where to sign up." Greer laughed, the sound easing the knot still lodged in her ribs. They drifted away just as silently as they had appeared.

"Drink," Alan murmured, materializing a fresh flute for her. Champagne smelled like apples and new beginnings. Across the room: Marco again, laughing with a critic, then angling a spotlight with the remote clipped to his belt. She felt steadier for that one constant person always in her peripheral vision.

CHARLES HENDERSON STOOD WITH EASY confidence. His laugh carried across the air like the clink of crystal glasses. His navy suit was impeccably tailored, his watch catching every stray beam of light. He looked entirely at home here, part of this glittering world of art and money, as natural as Marco weaving through the crowd.

Alan greeted him with genuine affection. "Charles, I'm so glad you could join us."

Charles returned the warmth for Alan, but when his eyes slid to Greer, his smile cooled.

Greer felt the dismissal keenly but kept her face neutral.

He acknowledged her with the barest nod, as though she were an afterthought, a nuisance in the way of a proper conversation. Greer managed a smile in return. Of course, he belonged here. Men like Charles always did. Wealth, confidence, control

—everything about him radiated it. Yet the under-current of disdain left Greer unsettled.

The hum rose—someone told a joke that made a small radius of people lift their faces like sunflowers. The caterers threaded through with trays. Greer took a long sip and let herself be a person instead of an assignment for three breaths.

When she drifted free, she noticed a man leaning against a column, sipping a cocktail, watching in earnest. An almost wistful expression on his face. He wore a shirt that might once have been ironed and a smile that had learned to make peace with itself. She'd left Alan talking to Charles Henderson, yet he seemed to appear beside her like magic. Alan greeted him warmly, clapping his shoulder. "Jasper Delaney! Back from hibernation."

Jasper's eyes flicked to Greer, warm, wry. "Where else would I be? You throw the kind of party that makes a man reconsider his work ethic."

"One day soon, Jasper, it'll be your turn," Alan said, with the kind of certainty Greer wished she could bottle.

Jasper tipped his glass in salute and chuckled. "Sure, Alan. One of these days."

He said it as a joke, but Greer heard the sober acceptance in his tone, a hint at an unspoken truth everyone knew but no one said aloud. With a nod, Jasper drifted back into the crowd.

The back of her neck prickled. Habit—not fear—made her scan the edges. Marco's absence announced itself again. She turned, slowly, not wanting to create a story where there wasn't one. Not at the bar. Not by the door. Not conferring near the track-light board. The kitchen door swung open, servers fanned out, and she almost caught sight of—nothing. Air. She filed it.

Alan folded her into a quick side-hug as if she were a lucky charm. "You're a sensation," he whispered. "Half the room has asked me who the woman in the pantsuit is, and the other half has already decided you're a legend." She snorted, which made him glow. "Just keep noticing," he added, as if he'd heard the page turning in her head.

Phoenix returned with a dignity incompatible with rumors he'd been in the kitchen. He wound through Greer's ankles and sat squarely on the runner like a sphinx. A guest crouched to take his picture; Phoenix tilted his head to his best side. Honestly, it was comical how their tabby cat had just been accepted by everyone as though he'd always been the gallery's mascot, and it had never been any other way.

By the time Alan had whisked her through a dozen more introductions—artists, critics, patrons —Greer's head swirled. The champagne sparkle of the evening was undercut by an undercurrent she couldn't quite name. Each face she'd met felt like a card in a hand she'd just been dealt.

But in that overly observant way of hers, the first impressions stuck like glue. Marco, warm, at ease, ever-present—until suddenly he wasn't. Vivian's ice-veiled disdain. Xavier's slick charm, too bright, too close. Charles's subtle dismissal. Dominic's silent, watchful, unreadable weight.

There were just too many observations, personalities, and little details that she'd picked up throughout the evening that she was exhausted. Who would have thought that standing around and looking engaged could wear you out? Large events always left her feeling like she'd survived a triathlon. Survive being the key sentiment. Under it all, there was that hint of pride reminding her she still had what it took to smile her way through an evening like this.

It was over.

Thank the heavens.

THE GALLERY BELOW WAS LOCKED AND DARK; THE hum of the night finally settled. Upstairs, the loft glowed golden from the old lamp on the end table, its shade leaning just enough to make the room feel like it had tilted into comfort. Greer had showered the champagne and perfume haze from her skin, slipped into soft joggers and a borrowed sweater. Her feet were tucked under her, toes warm against the cushion, a glass of amaretto fizzing faintly in her hand.

Alan dropped onto the other end of the couch, barefoot, hair damp, still somehow looking like he was about to take a bow. He held a glass of something amber that caught the light like honey. Phoenix had claimed the middle cushion, sprawled between them with an air of entitlement, his paws twitching in a dream.

Alan let out a long breath. "Well," he said, clinking his glass gently against hers, "we did it. Full house, no one fainted, no fistfights. Even Rivera kept his temper in check. That's success in my book."

Greer laughed. "You made it look effortless."

"I made it look expensive," Alan corrected, grinning. "Effortless was all Marco." He stretched, glanced at the cat, and added, "Though I'll let Phoenix claim partial credit. He knew exactly when to saunter in. Timing is everything."

Greer swirled her drink, thinking of the whirl of faces and compliments. "Jasper surprised me," she said at last. "He had that… ease, like he wasn't competing for anything. I liked him."

Alan smiled into his glass. "Everyone likes Jasper. He's brilliant when he feels like it. Trouble is, he doesn't often feel like it. I've shown his pieces a dozen times over the years, but he's never managed enough for a solo. The man's muse has a wicked sense of humor—comes and goes at will."

"Is he content with that?" Greer asked.

Alan considered. "Content enough. He's charming, easy company. But you can see it sometimes, the way his eyes flick toward Rivera or Vivian, like he's measuring a distance he doesn't want to admit exists."

They sipped in silence for a moment, listening to the faint tick of pipes settling.

"And Xavier?" Greer asked. "I couldn't decide if he was dazzling or… exhausting."

Alan barked a laugh. "Both. That's his brand. He's been around forever, the slickest salesman you'll ever meet. He can talk you into buying the shirt off your own back if he decides it's 'a piece worth saving.' People underestimate him because he's so flamboyant, but he's built three galleries on sheer charisma. He knows everybody, sells to every-body, and owes everybody a favor. He's like confetti —annoying, glittering, impossible to shake off."

"Does he drive you crazy?"

"Constantly," Alan said cheerfully. "But he also brings buyers through my doors. Half the pieces that sold tonight, Xavier nudged someone my way. He can't help himself. He loves the game more than the prize."

Greer tucked her chin against her knees, smil-ing. "You all know each other so well. It's like watching a troupe—everyone has their part."

"Mm." Alan took a thoughtful sip. "Some of us longer than others. Charles Henderson, for instance. Oldest client I've got. He's been buying since I opened, though never loudly. Modest check-book, impeccable taste. He bought that Rivera trip-tych tonight, by the way. Has the perfect wall for it in his Pacific Heights place."

"Of course he does," Greer murmured,

picturing him blending into the crowd, unremarkable until someone pointed.

Alan nodded. "Then there are the Sinclairs. Vivian and her late husband were fixtures for years. She kept at it after he passed, but her style... sharper now. She buys less, competes more. Still, when she does buy, it's always something bold. Tonight she lingered over the graphite-cut canvas. I wouldn't be surprised if she calls in the morning."

Greer tilted her head. "And the biggest client tonight?"

Alan's grin softened. "The Latimers, hands down. Old money, impeccable connections, and they adore Rivera. They've collected him since his Barcelona days. They bought the centerpiece. That alone paid for the whole event twice over."

"Does that happen often?"

"Often enough that I breathe easier when they RSVP," he said. "They're the kind of clients who keep the lights on. And the kind who invite you to their Tahoe chalet at Christmas to drink cognac you can't afford to sniff."

Greer laughed, leaning back against the couch. "Quite a life you've built here."

Alan tipped his head toward her, mock-serious. "And now you're part of it. No refunds, no returns."

Phoenix chose that moment to roll onto his back, paws splayed, belly shamelessly exposed. Alan set his empty glass on the coffee table and scratched between his ears. "See? Even he knows. You belong."

Greer smiled into her drink, letting the warmth settle. For once, she didn't argue.

FOURTEEN

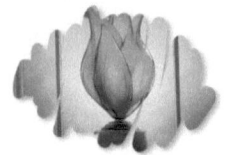

Greer jolted awake as Phoenix leaped onto her chest, his usually pliant body now stiff with tension. The tabby's ears lay flat against his head, his tail a bottlebrush of agitation. An eerie, guttural hiss tore from his throat, ancient and primal, raising goosebumps along Greer's arms.

"Phoenix, what is your malfunction?" Greer muttered groggily, her tongue thick with sleep. Trust her cat to go full-on demon mode at oh dark thirty in the morning. In all their time together, she'd never seen him like this. Another hiss, more insistent this time, propelled her upright. The air crackled with an ominous energy, every nerve in Greer's body screaming danger.

Years of crashing in various hotels all over the world had honed Greer's instincts to a razor's edge. But this felt different. Sinister. A suffocating stillness, like the calm before an earthquake. Heart slamming against her ribs, Greer slid out of bed, the chill of the hardwood a stark contrast to the adrenaline scorching her veins. The unmistakable sound of shattering glass from the gallery below froze the blood in her veins. Their home, their haven—violated.

She called 9-1-1 and gave them the details, hoping they'd send the cavalry but not expecting much, then stalked over to Alan's room.

"Alan!" Greer's urgent whisper shattered the silence as she slapped on his bedroom door, her shaking hand unable to form a fist. Why hadn't the security system sounded?

"Alan, wake up! We've got trouble!"

The door burst open, revealing a disheveled Alan, his normally impeccable silk pajamas askew.

"Jesus, Greer, this better be life or death!" he grumbled, rubbing the sleep from his eyes.

"Intruder alert," Greer hissed through clenched teeth, adrenaline surging through her veins. She fought the urge to reach for Alan's hand, to anchor herself in his steadying presence. Nothing in her life had prepared her for this kind of invasion of her sanctuary.

Alan's eyes narrowed, a steely resolve settling over his features. He snatched a gaudy ceramic vase from the side table, its garish hues clashing with the severity of the moment. Greer couldn't suppress a snort at the thought of confronting hardened criminals with a kitschy knick-knack. Her mother's disapproving voice echoed in her mind, chiding her for the absurdity of the situation.

As they crept down the stairs, Greer's heart pounded against her ribs, each step a deafening creak in the eerie stillness. The intruder's rummaging abruptly ceased, the sudden silence more unnerving than the previous commotion. Greer's breath came in shallow gasps, her body coiled tight with fear and anticipation. She'd stared down the barrel of a gun before, but never in her own home, never with so much at stake.

Alan's knuckles turned white around the vase, his jaw clenched with determination. Greer's gaze darted to the makeshift weapon, a bubble of hysterical laughter threatening to escape her throat. They were in way over their heads, a travel writer and an art dealer playing at being heroes. He clearly wasn't awake if he thought a vase was going to do much.

The scene that greeted them in the gallery's backroom was straight out of a nightmare. Broken bits littered the floor; priceless works of art reduced to mere debris. Drawers hung open, their contents strewn about like the entrails of a gutted beast. The acrid stench of paint thinner burned Greer's nostrils, mingling with the metallic tang of fear in her throat.

"Crikey," Greer breathed, her voice barely above a whisper. She reached for Alan's arm, needing to feel his solid presence beside her. "They've destroyed everything. What the frack were they looking for?"

Alan's lips thinned, his expression a mixture of rage and devastation.

"I don't know, but they're going to pay for this. Every last one of them."

Fists clenched, Greer scanned the wreckage—glass, splinters, a pattern hidden in the chaos. *This wasn't vandalism. It was a warning.* Something about the way the drawers were left open—not ransacked, but deliberately displayed—made her skin crawl.

The cobalt blue. Her pulse jumped. It was the same shade she'd seen by the mural that night, fresh and out of place. And the noise in the alley… she'd brushed it off as a fluke, a clatter in the dark. But what if it had been a signal? A message?

She'd been so focused on resettling her life, on guarding her heart, she hadn't recognized the signs. Not just a break-in. This was calculated. Personal. And she'd missed the first hint of it all.

As if whoever did this wanted them to see something... or someone. Her pulse kicked into overdrive.

Alan's face had gone ghostly pale, his eyes wide with disbelief. "Holy spit, Greer. Whoever did this wasn't messing around." He ran a trembling hand through his hair, a haunted expression flickering across his features. Was that a glimmer of guilt she detected, or perhaps a hint of fear?

Something about Alan's reaction didn't sit right with her. Though friends for such a short time, she could read him like a book. He was holding something back, putting up that familiar wall he always erected when he was trying to shield someone. But who was he protecting? And from what?

Greer sucked in a breath, trying to steady her nerves. "Alan, we have to wait for the police. Let's go sit in your office."

He nodded, fumbling for his phone with shaky hands. "Yeah, you're right. Let's do it."

As the first rays of dawn crept through the windows, the gallery buzzed with activity. Police officers swarmed the scene, their radios crackling with chatter. Greer hung back, wrapping her arms around herself as a whirlwind of emotions crashed over her. Relief battled with unease as she watched Alan pacing back and forth, his usually carefree demeanor replaced by a raw vulnerability she rarely witnessed.

Greer's skin prickled with anxiety, the presence of so many unfamiliar faces setting her nerves on edge. The chaos was suffocating, and every instinct urged her to flee to the safety of their apartment, to seek comfort in Phoenix's warm purrs. But abandoning Alan wasn't an option. Not now.

A tall man in a dark suit strode into the gallery like a force of nature, his chiseled features etched with determination. His piercing gaze swept the room, assessing every detail with laser-sharp focus. Greer couldn't help but notice the way his tailored suit clung to his broad shoulders, a testament to his disciplined lifestyle.

"Detective Burman, Special Crimes," he introduced himself, his deep voice resonating through the space. He flashed his badge with a practiced flick of the wrist, the gold glinting under the harsh fluorescent lights.

Greer watched as Alan visibly tensed, his usually unflappable demeanor cracking under the weight of Kyle's presence. His fingers twitched at his sides, a telltale sign of his unease.

"Kyle," Alan breathed, his tone a mix of surprise and something more tender, almost wistful. "I never thought I'd see you again. Not like this."

CHAPTER

FIFTEEN

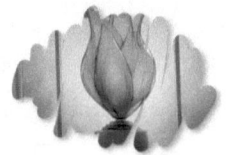

The air between them practically sizzled with unspoken history. Greer made a mental note to dig deeper into their past, her curiosity piqued.

"Alan," Kyle acknowledged, his voice carefully neutral, but Greer caught the way his eyes lingered on Alan's tousled hair and rumpled clothes a moment too long. "Wish I could say this was a social call, but we both know better."

Greer bit her tongue, resisting the urge to pepper them both with questions. The tension was palpable, a live wire of unresolved issues and barely contained attraction. She filed away every micro expression, every loaded glance, her mind whirring with possibilities.

Kyle turned his attention to the wreckage, his brows furrowing as he surveyed the destruction. "Any idea what they were after? This level of damage suggests they were looking for something specific."

Greer's gaze flicked to the broken sculpture—its hollow base cracked wide. It had been heavy enough to hide something. Had someone been storing secrets in plain sight?

Alan hesitated, a split second of indecision that spoke volumes to Greer. She knew him well enough now to recognize when he was holding something back, a skill honed from living in such close quarters.

"No clue," Alan replied, his voice a bit too steady, his nonchalance a tad too practiced. "I mean, we've got some valuable pieces, but nothing that would warrant this kind of violence."

Greer's *BS* detector pinged, her instincts screaming that Alan wasn't telling the whole truth. More questions dropped into place, forming a picture far more complicated than a simple break-in. She had a sinking feeling that Kyle, with his cop's intuition and personal history with Alan, sensed it too.

Alan's fingers nervously twisted the belt of his

robe into knots. "Honestly, Kyle, there's nothing of real value back here right now." His words hung in the air, the deception palpable and suffocating.

Alan was lying through his teeth and doing a piss-poor job of it. She'd watched him charm his way through high-stakes art sales without so much as a batted eyelash. What could rattle her normally unshakable roommate like this?

Detective Burman's eyebrow shot up, his voice dripping with skepticism. "Really? No hidden treasures squirreled away? No hush-hush deliveries at ungodly hours?"

Alan's back stiffened, his voice cracking as he fired back, "What is this, some dime-store detective novel? Give me a break, Kyle."

Greer winced at the raw defensiveness in Alan's tone. He was distant and cold, not his warm and charming self. This was more than a simple break-in. This was personal, the kind of personal that cut deep.

Her gaze pinged between them. Every breath buzzed with electricity. Fury? Regret? Longing?

Detective Burman's shoulders sagged, his voice softening. "Alan, I'm here to help. But if you're not giving me the full picture…"

"I am," Alan snapped, cutting him off. But the slight tremor in his words told a different story.

A frigid unease gripped Greer's core. She'd made her living deciphering the unsaid, detecting the subtle shifts in inflection and body language. And in this moment? Every journalistic instinct screamed that Alan's perfectly polished veneer was cracking, revealing the deception beneath.

The two men continued their charged exchange, the air thick with unspoken history. Detective Burman's gaze bored into Alan, searching for chinks in his armor. Alan squirmed under the intensity, a flush creeping up his neck and staining his cheeks.

Jeebus, the electricity arcing between them could illuminate the entire city block. And here she was, the awkward third wheel in the midst of their unfolding drama. Typical Greer, forever stumbling into the tangled web of other people's complicated relationships.

Greer cleared her throat, the sound unnaturally loud in the tense quiet. "So, should I start cleaning up this mess, or…?"

They spun to face her, startled, as if they'd forgotten her existence. Detective Burman shook his head, his white-knuckled grip on his notepad relaxing a fraction. "Not yet. We still need to process the scene."

Their voices lowered to a whisper, leaving Greer to marinate in her own tumultuous thoughts. She'd faced down a mother-in-law on the warpath with less apprehension than she felt witnessing this bizarre tango between Alan and the detective. Something about their dynamic felt… off-kilter.

A few minutes later, the detective stormed out.

The gallery, once her refuge, had morphed into a labyrinth of unanswered questions. Between the assault on Alan, this baffling break-in, and the electrifying chemistry between him and the detective, Greer's mind reeled with disjointed pieces of a puzzle that stubbornly refused to fit together.

Her hands itched for action. She thrived when cracking codes, but this wasn't folklore—it was personal. This wasn't some far-flung town with ancient traditions to decipher. This was her home, her best friend, and nothing about this situation made a lick of sense. And it was slipping through her fingers.

One thing was abundantly clear. The Bayside Art Collective concealed more secrets than she'd anticipated. Collapsing onto a plush velvet sofa, Greer's clammy palms gripped her knees as she watched Alan prowl back and forth, his robe tangling around his restless limbs. He paced like a caged tiger, and Greer couldn't shake the gnawing dread that they were all in way over their heads.

"This is absolutely nuts," Greer muttered, her gaze sweeping the ransacked room. "Who would do something like this to the gallery?"

Alan's shoulders slumped as he stopped short. His voice quavered, revealing his distress. "In the art world, honey, the list of potential culprits is longer than a harlot's little black book. Cutthroat rivals, pissed-off painters, even unhinged collectors."

Greer's eyes narrowed. "Even Xavier?"

Alan winced. "Especially Xavier. That man's dodged enough fraud accusations to qualify for sainthood—or federal prison."

The waver in Alan's words sent ice through her veins. Something about this whole situation didn't add up.

"Alan," Greer's voice was soft but resolute, "it's time to level with me. Right now."

Alan turned to face her, the morning sun glinting off his earring and casting shadows across his face. "Greer, sweetie," he said, his usual confidence wavering, "I don't even know how to begin explaining this mess."

But Alan always had a flair for storytelling, launching into vivid details at the drop of a hat. This hesitation, this uncertainty, felt completely out of character.

"Okay, first step. Let's get ourselves cleaned up and properly caffeinated," Greer suggested. "We can't face this mess without our wits about us."

Alan nodded, his hands trembled noticeably as he headed out of the gallery and up to their apartment, his mind clearly elsewhere.

Greer traipsed behind him, her brain already parsing every detail, every nuance. It was how she always started her stories, collecting thoughts, assembling questions. But this was not some random interview subject. Maintaining her usual professional detachment was impossible.

Two hours later, they sat in Alan's office, the aroma of fresh coffee battling the lingering stench of fear. Police tape blocked off the backroom, a stark reminder of the intrusion. Phoenix was locked upstairs for now. The last thing they needed was him down here prowling and getting tangled in something broken.

Greer's fingers fidgeted against her mug. The

garish yellow tape taunted her need for control, for order. She should be hot on the trail of her next story. Instead, she was mired in this chaos, watching her friend come apart at the seams.

Marco poked his head in as the last officer left. "What happened here?"

"Break-in. Early this morning," Alan answered, his voice level despite his fingers drumming restlessly on the desk. "Take today off, Marco. The gallery's staying closed."

Marco nodded curtly, glancing warily around the room before silently following the uniformed officers out.

Alan slumped into his chair, his fingers drumming an anxious rhythm as he arranged for the alley door's replacement again. Greer's mind spun with the morning's events, but her thoughts scattered as Phoenix sauntered in, his tail held high despite his quivering whiskers. At least someone was keeping their cool.

The tabby jumped into Greer's lap, his purrs vibrating against her thighs. She'd barely begun to relax when Phoenix stiffened, his body coiled with tension. His ears swiveled forward, alert and focused, as he leaped onto Alan's desk. With a menacing growl, he pawed urgently at a drawer, his claws scratching against the wood.

"Good grief, Phoenix?" Greer muttered, unsure what to expect as she watched the cat's bizarre behavior. Her mind shifted into analytical mode, cataloging every detail of his posture and movements. Life had taught her to trust her gut when something felt off.

Alan's hands fumbled as he yanked open the drawer, his face draining of color as he reached inside. Greer's heart raced at the sudden shift in his demeanor. He looked utterly wrecked. When she glimpsed the small recording device, its red light blinking ominously, her blood ran cold.

"Judas priest," Alan whispered hoarsely. "I've been recording my calls, just in case, but I forgot all about this."

With trembling fingers, he pressed play. Each blasted revelation tilted Greer's world further off its axis. Kyle's grim warnings. Chilling threats from unknown callers. Vivian Sinclair's biting accusations of stolen war art. And through it all, the threads of Alan's grandfather's wartime dealings, weaving the past and present into a tangled web of secrets someone might kill to keep buried. Who knew what? And what exactly did they know? Or think they knew?

Greer's head spun, a terrifying picture forming. "Jeebus, Alan," she breathed, her heart pounding. "What have you gotten yourself into?"

Alan sagged into his chair, his usual vibrance extinguished, replaced by raw, unadulterated terror. Greer's protective instincts roared to life. Alan was more than just her roommate—he was family now, the only person besides Phoenix she truly trusted, and someone was threatening him. The gallery's shadows loomed around them, suddenly sinister and oppressive.

"I think the real question, darling," Alan rasped, his icy, quivering fingers finding hers, "is what have I gotten you into?"

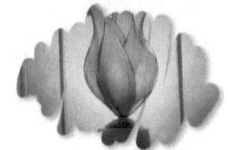

The glow from Alan's desk lamp danced across the invaluable paintings, transforming the once-stately office into a scene from a thriller. Greer's nose wrinkled as the familiar scent of aged canvas mingled with an undercurrent of decay. Her hands trembled slightly as she traced the antique desk, doubt creeping into her mind. The assault. The gallery's finances. Three break-ins in as many months, and the nagging suspicion that someone had it out for Alan made her question her own capabilities as his protector.

Her thoughts spiraled—none of the answers were comforting. She'd handled worse on paper, but this was real, and she had nothing solid to hold on to.

Earlier, she'd caught Marco fidgeting nervously by the security door, his phone glued to his ear. He kept glancing over his shoulder mid-whisper. It set off the same internal alarms that had prompted her to read Peter's emails.

The information stubbornly refused to connect, like a brain teaser with missing clues. Every fiber of her investigative being told her Marco was hiding something big.

"Hey Marco, you good?" Greer kept her tone light, masking her suspicion despite the desert in her mouth.

Marco let out a strained chuckle. "Oh, you know, just the usual grind."

She'd made small talk with enough shady characters to spot a deflection from a mile away. Her muscles tensed, expecting the flaccid excuses so common with people not being up front.

"You've been off your game recently."

"Nah, it's nothing. Just some personal stuff," Marco blurted out, shoving his phone in his pocket as he bolted.

Greer's hand twitched, yearning for her trusty notebook to jot down every detail of Marco's bizarre behavior. His shifty demeanor set off the same warning bells she'd felt right before learning about her husband's intentions to divorce her.

"What's on your mind, Greer?" Alan's normally vibrant voice sounded strained. The alley ambush and the latest break-in had left lines of worry on his face that made him the spitting image of his late dad.

Snapping back to the present, Greer's heart raced. "I can't shake the feeling we're missing something crucial."

As Alan opened his mouth to respond, a blur of fur streaked across the room, nearly sending a delicate vase crashing. Phoenix had appointed himself lead detective on the case. With feline grace, he leapt onto the desk, then back off again, scattering papers in his wake.

"Gotta love that fur ball," Alan chuckled, his fondness clear as day. "Thinks he's the next Sherlock Holmes."

Greer's lips curled into a smirk, the tension easing for a moment. "Oh, he's got a sixth sense for trouble, alright. If only untangling this web were as easy as following his hunches."

Phoenix yowled and bolted out the door, claws scraping wood.

Greer froze. "He wants us to follow," she said, tension wrapping tight around her spine.

Alan shrugged, but the tremor in his hands didn't escape Greer's eye.

"Someone's out there," Greer hissed, her pulse thundering in her ears.

They crept through the gallery's eerie shadows, tracking Phoenix as he wove between unsettling sculptures and watchful paintings. Each creak of the floorboards beneath their feet frayed Greer's already taut nerves.

The realization that they had an invader in the gallery two nights in a row spoke of sheer determination and escalating desperation. Drawing closer, they caught the unmistakable cadence of Marco's voice.

"You think I'm running a charity here, Jasper? No payment, no product."

"We've gotta move fast, Marco. Tonight's the night," another man insisted, his voice low and urgent. "If we don't act now, it's game over."

Greer's gut twisted. *Product?* What was he selling? It sounded less like art and more like a transaction he couldn't afford to get caught in.

She strained to catch every word, her mind whirring like a supercomputer. Jasper's tone,

Marco's demands. Her stomach churned. Were they working together? She glanced at Alan, their eyes meeting in a moment of grim understanding. They kept listening, Greer trying to make sense of the tangled web, until the two men slipped out the back door and vanished into the night.

Phoenix rubbed against Greer's legs, his soft purrs a momentary comfort amidst the chaos. She stooped, running her fingers through his fur, finding a sliver of peace in his steady presence.

Back in the office, Alan slumped into his chair, twisting one of his dad's tacky rings. "I never asked for any of this, Greer. The gallery, the expectations, it was all Dad's thing." His words came out shaky, years of bottled-up resentment finally spilling over. "I wanted to be on the force, like Kyle. But Gramps, then my dad, they put their whole cursed life into this place. How could I crush those dreams? Now I'm trapped here, jumping at every noise, weighed down by whatever is going on."

Alan's raw anguish sucker-punched Greer right in the gut. His desperate need to break free from the family chains resonated deep within her soul. Hadn't she spent years fighting tooth and nail to blaze her own trail, defying everyone's expectations to chase her globetrotting dreams?

She reached across the battle-scarred mahogany desk, the one Alan's grandfather had excitedly picked out when he first set up shop, and clasped his trembling hand.

"Hey, listen to me. You've poured your heart and soul into this place, and there's no way I'm going to sit by and let anything happen to it."

Alan let out a weary sigh as he reached for the phone. The weight of countless sacrifices bearing down on him. "I've gotta make some calls."

Greer's heart clenched as she watched her best friend's broad shoulders sag under the crushing burden. She knew that bone-tired look all too well. The gallery was more than just a building to Alan's family—it was their legacy. And here he was, desperately trying to keep the ship afloat while she stood by, powerless to do anything.

"I'm gonna head up and throw together something to eat. Just don't hide out down here all night, okay?" She gave his hand one last squeeze, her thumb brushing against his knuckles in their unspoken 'I got your back' gesture. The least she could do was stand by his side, even if she couldn't magically fix everything.

Alan gave a distracted nod, his gaze fixed on the desk calendar as the setting sun cast ominous shadows across tomorrow's date. His restless fingers traced the well-worn leather, a nervous habit born from one too many tough decisions made at this very desk. The unspoken question hung heavy in the air—would this be the battle that finally broke him?

SEVENTEEN

The next morning, Alan unlocked the gallery doors with an air of unease, his usual bravado notably absent. Greer watched him with a heavy heart, hating the helplessness that gnawed at her insides. She yearned to protect him, to solve this mystery, and make everything right again. But life wasn't a deuced Nancy Drew novel. Some problems couldn't be fixed with a clever quip and a magnifying glass.

"I'm gonna grab us some lunch," Greer announced, desperate to escape the suffocating tension. "Back in a flash."

The autumn air bit at her skin. Alan—steady, sure Alan—was cracking. And with him, so was her sense of solid ground.

She should be at her computer, crafting elegant prose about the newest restaurant or cafe. Instead, she was hunting for clues in her own backyard. Maybe she'd been naïve to think she could ever truly have a home without it being threatened.

Fallen leaves crunched beneath her feet, their whispers echoing the secrets that hung in the air. Shadows stretched across the pavement, transforming familiar storefronts into looming, mysterious entities. The once-friendly neighborhood seemed to mock her. How could everything look so normal when their lives were unraveling faster than a cheap sweater?

Greer ducked into the music store next door, determined to find some answers. The owner, a blue-haired pixie with an arsenal of snark, looked up from her inventory.

"Hey, you're from the gallery, right?" The girl quirked an eyebrow. "Please tell me you're not responsible for that god-awful neon monstrosity they put up last month. I swear, it looked like a radioactive pretzel mated with a disco ball."

Despite the gravity of the situation, Greer couldn't help but snort. "Nah, that's all Alan's doing. The man's never met a color he didn't like."

For a fleeting moment, the knot in her chest

loosened. She could almost picture Alan's mischievous grin as he unveiled his latest avant-garde acquisition, daring anyone to question his artistic vision. Alan really could brighten even the gloomiest day with his infectious enthusiasm and zest for life.

Greer gnawed on her lip, the taste of copper in her mouth as she fought to banish the haunting image of Alan lying battered on the unforgiving pavement that fateful evening. The memory clung to her like a stubborn cobweb, refusing to release its grip. A shudder rippled through her body, the chill of that evening forever etched into her bones.

As she continued her interviews, Greer's mind whirred with each new piece of information. An undercurrent pulsed beneath the seemingly disconnected incidents, hinting at a darkness she couldn't quite grasp.

Her notebook quickly filled with hastily scribbled observations—a shadowy figure skulking near the gallery's rear entrance, whispers of a heated disagreement between rival artists. While not concrete leads, Greer could see that an invisible thread wove through these tales, binding them together in a sinister tapestry.

Balancing burritos and a heavy heart, Greer

stepped into the gallery, only to find Alan pacing restlessly, his usually immaculate appearance in shambles. His rumpled shirt and haphazard tie spoke volumes about the turmoil raging within, the dark circles beneath his eyes a testament to the sleepless nights that plagued him. Greer's heart constricted at the sight of her friend so visibly shaken.

Alan whirled to face her, a manic glint in his eye. "Greer, it's Vincent. It all comes back to that ingrate."

"Whoa, hold up. Your ex-boyfriend Vincent?" Greer's eyebrows practically hit her hairline. "What's he got to do with this?"

Slumping into his chair, Alan's fingers absently traced the worn edge of his desk, a nervous tic that betrayed his inner struggle. "Vincent could never stomach my success with the gallery. He's a really good artist, but he just couldn't make it to the top." Alan's voice cracked. "When I ended things, he swore he'd make me pay for 'holding him back.' And slap me sideways, even after everything he's put me through, deep down in some idiotic part of me, he still matters."

"Alan, I thought you guys ended things a year ago? That seems like a long time to hold a grudge."

Alan shrugged, his mouth drawn in a thin line.

Greer mulled over Alan's revelation as he spoke. *Could all the drama be the workings of a jilted ex with an axe to grind?* Her mind couldn't put all the disconnected details into a coherent narrative. Though this situation felt unnervingly familiar.

"Are you thinking Vincent's in cahoots with Marco and Jasper?" The gears in Greer's head spun into overdrive. "That maybe he's using his art world connections to mastermind these heists."

Alan's eyes grew wide, a flicker of hurt dancing across his face. "Wouldn't put it past him. The man's a master manipulator. But Marco and Jasper? I'm not so sure."

EIGHTEEN

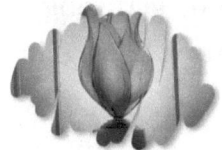

The practiced diplomat in her wanted to soften the blow. She'd learned the hard way that sometimes the ugliest theories proved true. How many times had her skepticism saved her from sticky situations in the past?

Greer tilted her head, staring out into space, recalling her earlier run-ins with Marco and the hushed conversation they'd overheard between him and Jasper.

"We're gonna need more proof before we jump to any conclusions," she muttered.

A sudden motion caught Greer's attention, yanking her gaze away from Alan's intense stare. These days, the slightest unexpected movement set her on edge, a side effect of too much time spent looking over her shoulder. *Blasted*! When had she become such a jumpy mess? Phoenix was up to his old tricks, tail lashing with purpose as he stalked towards the back of the gallery.

"Alan," she said, gesturing toward their feline guide. "Call me crazy, but I think Sherlock Paws is onto something."

They crept after Phoenix, weaving through the maze of artwork. Each cautious footfall hammered home the gravity of the situation. The air grew thicker the deeper they ventured, the comforting aroma of vintage canvases and lemon polish. Phoenix's insistent meows led them to the rear of the storeroom. The cat pawed furiously at a grime-encrusted shipping crate wedged under an ancient sculpture, clearly untouched for quite some time. Funny, it felt oddly rational for them to tail a cat through a dusty storage area. Together, they heaved the crate free and eased it to the ground.

Tucked beneath the crate, something glinted— foil, maybe? Greer stooped to pick it up. A gallery business card, singed at the edge. Handwritten on the back: "You don't deserve this place."

As Alan hunted for a crowbar to pry loose the weathered boards, hands shaking almost imperceptibly, Greer watched Phoenix prowl the perimeter, ever the vigilant sentinel.

"Holy Forking Shirtballs! This whole time, that crafty fur ball's been trying to lead us here," she mused, rewarding Phoenix with a scritch behind the ears, welcoming the distraction for her restless fingers.

Alan cracked a smile, but Greer spotted the creases of concern around his eyes as his rings caught the faint light. Those baubles could probably cover her rent for a decade. She made a mental note to get the story behind them later. When they weren't knee-deep in a potential family scandal.

"Looks like our little furry gumshoe is onto something. Think we should make him an official member of the team?" Alan's attempt at a joke fell flat, unable to hide the quiver in his words.

A genuine laugh escaped Greer. "Guess he's earned his keep after all. Been busting his tail since the start."

Her trademark skepticism had taken a rare backseat. Alan was a true-blue pal, a rarity in her world of far-flung adventures and fleeting connections.

"Little help here?" Alan wedged the crowbar into the crate's stubborn lid. Greer's mind shifted into problem-solving mode. She snagged a stray plank and jammed it into the widening gap, their efforts falling into sync with surprising ease.

Suddenly, a scrape from the gallery froze them in place. The sound kick-started Greer's pulse into overdrive. Footsteps cut through the silence with unsettling purpose. Greer's chest tightened—she knew that stride, the walk of someone used to owning the room.

That old familiar tension seized her shoulders, the same unease that crept in when a stranger invaded her space on a packed train. Her finely tuned danger radar, courtesy of one too many solo trips to sketchy locales, blared a warning.

Alan set the crowbar on the crate and slipped out to face their mystery visitor. His rigid posture betrayed his nerves, despite the well-practiced grin plastered on his face.

"Well, well, Alan. Fancy catching you here," Xavier drawled, his honeyed words dripping with insincerity.

Greer's skin crawled at the sound, her bullshit detector blaring like a foghorn. She'd encountered more than her fair share of con artists during her travels, and Xavier's act reeked of the same deception.

Alan's shoulders tensed, his jaw clenching as he faced the intruder. "To what do I owe this unexpected pleasure in *my* gallery?"

Xavier sauntered into the gallery like he owned the place, his eyes roving over the artwork with a calculating gleam. "Oh, you know me. Always on the hunt for inspiration. And I must say, your collection is quite… evocative. I was hoping to catch up with Marco."

Greer's fingers itched to wipe that smug grin off Xavier's face. The way his gaze lingered on certain pieces, sizing them up like a jewel thief casing a mark. Every nerve screamed at her to step in, to put herself between Alan and this snake in the grass. But she held her ground, trusting Alan to handle his own turf.

"I appreciate the compliment, but it's time we closed for the evening." Alan's words were polite, but the steel beneath them was unmistakable. He shifted subtly, blocking Xavier's path deeper into the gallery.

Xavier's chuckle set Greer's teeth on edge. "Come now, Alan. Surely you can make an exception for an old friend? For old times' sake?" His smile was all sharp edges and empty charm.

Greer's heart raced as Xavier took a step closer,

the space between the two men shrinking to a hair's breadth. She caught Alan's eye, a thousand unspoken words passing between them in an instant.

"I'm afraid I really must insist." Alan's voice never wavered, but Greer spotted the telltale twitch of his hand, betraying his unease. "Perhaps we could schedule a tour during business hours?"

Xavier opened his mouth to retort, but a sudden crash from the back room cut him off. His head snapped towards the sound, eyes narrowing to slits. "What was that?" he snarled, all pretense of civility vanishing.

Greer's body coiled like a spring, ready to leap into action at a moment's notice. The hair on the back of her neck stood at attention, every sense on high alert. She'd relied on those instincts to get her out of more than one close call in life.

Alan let out a strained laugh that fooled no one. "Ah, that'll be Phoenix up to his usual antics. Never met a vase he didn't want to topple."

Greer knew Alan needed backup, stat. Sure, their friendship was greener than a novice hiker's boots, but she'd rather square off against a pack of rabid hyenas than leave him high and dry. Xavier should be a cakewalk in comparison.

Her heart jack-hammered against her ribs as she watched Alan's shoulders hunch, his fingers compulsively fiddling with his sleeve cuff—the tell-tale sign of his mounting anxiety she'd clocked from day one. Seeing him cornered like this? Unacceptable.

Thinking fast, Greer seized the momentary chaos and darted to Alan's side, her mouth desert-dry. "There you are," she chirped, looping her arm through his. She felt him tense at her touch, then relax into her, like she was his lifeline in a churning sea. "Ready to hit that new tapas joint?"

Xavier's hawk-like stare zeroed in on Greer, suspicion and surprise battling for dominance on his angular face. The gallery's unforgiving light cast harsh shadows across his features. "Ms. Caldwell."

"Mr. Delacroix. Nice seeing you again," she replied without hesitation, thrusting out her hand and praying it wouldn't betray her nerves. "I'm sorry, but we're running late. We've got a date with an oversized sangria."

The instant Xavier's cold, clammy palm met hers, her skin crawled. Shaking his hand dredged up queasy memories of wrangling unsavory specimens in her college anthropology classes. At least those relics had the decency to stay buried.

Begrudgingly, Xavier released her hand, his grip a smidge too vise-like for comfort. Alan smoothly angled them towards the exit.

"Another time, Xavier," he managed, his voice strained beneath the forced levity. "Let's do drinks and reminisce about the good old days, yeah?"

CHAPTER
NINETEEN

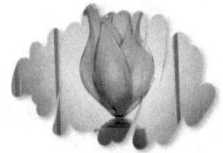

They all but strong-armed Xavier out the door, Alan throwing the deadbolt with a jarring clunk. Greer's guts churned as they double-timed it down the sidewalk, the night air searing her lungs. In the tomblike silence, their footfalls ricocheted like gunshots. Only once they careened around the corner did Alan let out a shaky exhale.

"Jeez, that was way too close," he breathed, engulfing her in a crushing hug.

Greer held on to Alan like he was the only solid thing in a world turned upside down. Years of keeping everyone at arm's length, and now here she was, clinging to her best friend as if her life depended on it. The intensity of her need to protect him knocked the wind out of her. When had he become so important to her? As they disentangled, a silent promise passed between them—they were in this together, no matter what other disaster awaited them.

"Alright, spill. What was with that pretentious prick?" Greer asked, trying to inject a little levity into the suffocating tension.

Alan let out a humorless chuckle, raking a hand through his disheveled hair. "Xavier Fluffing Delacroix. Slimeball art dealer with a talent for pushing boundaries and a hard-on for my gallery. I've had my eye on him for a while now."

Leave it to some bougie southern turd to stir up trouble. This had front-page scandal written all over it. Her reporter's nose twitched—there had to be a money trail, some dirt she could unearth. Burying herself in research sounded a whole lot more appealing than untangling this web they'd stumbled into.

They wandered the long way back to the gallery, taking random turns as if they could shake off the night's events. Greer's head buzzed with unanswered questions, each more unsettling than the last. But with Alan's solid presence beside her, she knew one thing for certain—whatever storm was brewing, they'd weather it together.

Back in the apartment, Greer swore under her breath, her nails digging into her palms as icy tendrils of dread crept up her spine. She should be doing more work on her next article. Instead, she was pacing her apartment like a caged animal. The universe clearly had a twisted sense of humor. The run-in with Xavier Delacroix had shaken her to the core, and now every shadow seemed to hold a hidden threat.

She whirled to face Alan, desperation etched into every line of her face. "We need to call in the big guns, Alan. Detective Burman, the cops, anyone who can handle this mess. We're in way over our heads here."

Alan shook his head vehemently, shoving his trembling hands into his pockets. "And watch our only leads disappear faster than free booze at a frat party? Not a chance."

Greer's logical side screamed in protest. She'd built her life on meticulous research and carefully calculated risks, not running half-cocked into danger like some adrenaline-junkie vigilante. But the thought of Alan facing this nightmare alone? Unthinkable.

She grabbed Alan by the shoulders, forcing him to meet her gaze. "What leads though? This isn't about some penny-ante art gallery break-in. And we have no idea what Marco and that Jasper guy were even talking about. There's something more going on here."

Alan's bravado crumbled like a sandcastle at high tide, the raw terror in his eyes impossible to miss. The walls of the apartment seemed to press in on them, the weight of their predicament suffocating.

"I'm terrified too," Greer confessed, her voice a strained whisper. She hugged herself tightly, a long-abandoned habit from the days following her father's death. "I haven't felt this scared in my life, but we can't keep burying our heads in the sand and hoping this blows over."

The admission tasted bitter on her tongue. She'd spent years cultivating an image of unflappable competence, yet here she stood, practically vibrating with anxiety. Just like that scared woman who'd watched helplessly as her marriage fractured apart.

Alan exhaled heavily, fingers raking through his hair. "I know you're right," he admitted gruffly. "Not like the police have done much about the stolen items I reported, or even about me being beaten in the alley. But the minute we tell Kyle, we're benched."

Control. That's what this boiled down to. Handing over the reins made her insides twist into knots. But maybe that was precisely why they had to do it. Dropping onto the couch next to Alan, Greer faced him.

"Okay, hear me out," she said, a wild idea taking root. "What if we set a trap of our own? Dangle some bait and reel in the sleazebag and then have the cops crash the party in the act?"

A familiar thrill raced through her veins, the same adrenaline rush that had fueled her through the upheaval of her personal life the year before.

A mischievous smirk slowly crept across Alan's face, even as his shoulders remained taut. "I like the way you think, doll. What's the plan?"

Before she could answer, her phone buzzed—an anonymous number. One line lit the screen: "Back off." No sender. No trail. Greer swallowed hard. This just got personal.

"We need a red herring, some kind of irresistible lure for our wannabe art thief," Greer proposed, anticipation sparking in her gut despite the ever-present knot of apprehension.

Alan's face lit up. "Ooh, I've got just the thing! What about that god-awful modern art monstrosity I snagged at the last estate sale?"

An unbidden laugh bubbled up from Greer's throat, bordering on manic. "Wait, you mean the one that looks like Cthulhu got busy with a Picasso? That'll work."

Alan clapped his hands together like a child waiting for dessert. "We'll start a rumor that it's a newly authenticated Nils Svenson masterpiece lost for decades. What art thief worth their salt could pass up a score like that?"

As they ironed out the details of their hare-brained scheme, a dizzying mix of anticipation and apprehension churned in Greer's stomach. They were wading into seriously dangerous waters here, but the chance to finally crack this case and nail the bastard responsible? Too tempting to pass up.

This whole thing was absolutely crazy. Greer knew it in her bones. But jeepers, if it didn't feel like every other wild ride she'd ever chased in the name of a juicy story. Only this time, the stakes were personal.

Alan sat back against the couch, studying her intently. "So, we're really doing this? This insane plan that'll either be our crowning glory or the final nail in our coffins?"

Greer shot him a crooked grin, adrenaline already buzzing through her system. "Hey, 'batty with a side of brilliance' is kind of our thing, isn't it?"

A WEEK HAD PASSED WITHOUT ANY NEW DRAMA, bringing them to the night of their off-the-books stakeout. Greer's nerves were strung so tight she was amazed they didn't twang like over-tuned guitar strings. Her heart hammered against her ribs, and her mouth tasted like she'd face-planted in a sand-box. This was precisely why she stuck to solo travel pieces. At least then she was the one calling the shots. But no, she had to play detective, with her best friend's future on the line, no less.

The gallery was dead silent, except for the occasional groan of old wood settling. Greer tucked herself behind an enormous abstract monstrosity, trying to ignore the Charley horse seizing up her leg. All those years of deciphering cultural subtleties on the fly had drilled one thing into her skull: the devil's in the details. One seemingly minor clue could crack a case wide open. Alan was hunkered down close by, his trademark man-bling conspicuously missing to avoid drawing any unwanted attention.

The minutes crawled by. Greer was wondering if she'd gone completely mental when the muffled scrape of metal on metal turned her blood to ice water in her veins. Her gut instinct just knew this story was about to take a hard left turn. She strained to hear past the blood pounding in her ears. Inch by inch, the front door creaked open, a dark figure slipping inside.

With the rear exit still sporting plywood couture courtesy of the last break-in, whoever this was had to have a key. So much for keeping this simple. Up until now, her life seemed like child's play compared to this. The list of potential perps was getting uncomfortably short, but their motives? Spinning out of control in a dozen different directions. Greer white-knuckled her phone, ready to speed-dial Burman, her head reeling at the rush of adrenaline.

TWENTY

The shadowy figure slipped past their carefully placed decoy, venturing deeper into the gallery. Greer's heart sank as she watched their meticulously orchestrated trap come apart at the seams. If her editor could see her now, hunkered down in the shadows like a discount store detective… Still, assuming she made it out of this alive, it would be one heck of a story. The crinkle of police tape whispered ominously, a stark reminder of just how much was at stake.

Alan's muffled voice came through the comm link. "It's go time, Greer."

"Not yet." She leaned in, breath tight, sweaty palm braced against the wall. The intruder had completely ignored the bait, making a beeline for the storeroom instead. Greer's stomach churned, a countdown to the looming confrontation.

The seconds ticked by at an agonizing pace, each one feeling like a sucker punch to Greer's already shot nerves. Searing pain ripped through her leg, the muscle cramping hard after being stuck in this pretzel position for so long. Nothing could have prepared her for the unique agony of an art gallery stakeout.

Suddenly, the lights snapped on, temporarily blinding Greer. Blinking furiously to clear the spots from her vision, she zeroed in on the figure crouched over the shipping crate—Marco. He looked like a cornered animal, his shaking hands clawing at the splintered wood. Marco was their culprit. While they had suspected him based on the growing evidence, her mind still struggled to accept that such a trusted member of the gallery really was involved.

Greer's thoughts spun. But Marco hadn't taken the bait—instead, he'd gone straight to that crate. That meant he knew what was hidden, and more importantly, who was still pulling the strings. So not part of the art thefts? Something more? The questions swirled without end.

"SFPD! Freeze!" Detective Burman's booming

voice echoed through the gallery, stopping Marco cold.

The barked order sent a jolt of adrenaline surging through Greer's veins. Every muscle in her body coiled, ready to run even as logic reminded her she wasn't the one in Burman's crosshairs.

Shock and rage battled for dominance on Marco's face, but beneath the bravado, Greer spotted a flicker of unadulterated fear. Adrenaline surging, she emerged from her hiding spot, Alan's reassuring presence at her side despite the almost imperceptible quiver in his hands.

This wasn't like documenting an upcoming parade or a new cafe. This was raw, personal betrayal playing out in real-time. Her fingers itched for her notepad. Some habits die hard, but she forced them still.

"You've been a busy boy, Marco," Alan said, his tone dripping with barely restrained venom. "What, did you think I wouldn't put two and two together?" The weight of shattered trust hung heavy in his words, the history of shared laughter and late-night brainstorming sessions now forever tainted.

Poor Alan. Her chest tightened, watching her friend's composure crack. Nothing compared to watching someone you trusted reveal their true colors.

Cornered, Marco's well-crafted mask crumbled, desperate fragments of excuses tumbling from his lips. Alan cut him off with a single, resolute gesture, his eyes mirroring the pain of a friendship reduced to ashes.

"It's over, Marco," Greer said, her voice unwavering even as her insides churned like a stormy sea.

She'd practiced that tone countless times in her life. Amazing how useful those skills proved now. In a matter of moments, the gallery was swarming with police officers.

Marco's gaze darted frantically, a caged animal seeking any means of escape. "You don't get it," he growled, his voice cracking under the strain. "This shit isn't mine!"

Such a predictable defense. The world had heard similar protests from smugglers in Southeast Asia to art thieves in Europe. Different accents, same desperation.

As the officers closed in, Marco's facade shattered completely. The crowbar clattered to the floor, the sound of his surrender echoing through the space. "Alright, alright! You want the whole freaking story? I'll give it to you!" His voice splintered, his meticulously maintained lies disintegrating in an instant.

Detective Burman questioned a handcuffed Marco, his shoulders sagging in defeat, while Alan and Greer listened intently just outside the door to the storage room. Greer could practically feel the tension rolling off Alan in waves, his breath shallow and tightly controlled.

She should take notes. This would make an excellent article. If she could ever write about it. But some stories weren't meant for public consumption, no matter how compelling the narrative.

The confession poured out of Marco like blood from an open wound.

"It was so bloomin' simple. Started a year back. We moved the product in batches every month, like clockwork. I worked with Xavier Delacroix. He handled getting the dope from point A to point B. Jasper's paintings, the abstract ones nobody wanted to look at twice, had a hidden compartment behind the canvas, just big enough to stash the coke packets. The drugs were practically invisible, tucked away behind the stretchers and frames. Nobody ever noticed a thing." His voice took on a hollow, detached quality with each word.

"Why?" Detective Burman asked, giving voice to the question on everyone's mind.

Marco's answer was barely audible, weighted down by guilt. "Jasper's art wasn't moving. And his habit was getting out of control. He needed the cash."

Greer shifted her stance, her gut instincts prickling. The same old story. Addiction leading to desperation leading to crime. But something about Marco's tone felt rehearsed, like he'd practiced this confession in front of a mirror.

"And Delacroix's role in all this?"

"Xavier's got cartel connections down in South America." Marco's words settled over the room like a toxic fog.

TWENTY-ONE

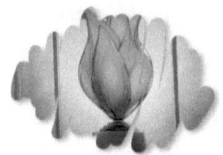

A shiver rippled through her shoulders. Of course, there'd be cartel involvement. Because apparently art galleries weren't dramatic enough without adding drug lords to the mix. She was already composing headlines she'd never write.

With a nod, he indicated a painting propped haphazardly in the corner, slated for display in the coming week. Marco's gaze lingered on the piece, his eyes haunted by the memories of countless identical shipments, each one dragging him deeper into the abyss.

The pristine gallery felt suffocating, each artwork a potential vessel for corruption. The many transactions she'd witnessed. How many of those conversations had been coded negotiations?

A uniformed officer flipped the painting over, running her fingers along the back. She paused, frowning at a slight unevenness. With a curt nod from Detective Burman, she carefully pried open the frame, revealing a small, crinkled plastic packet nestled inside. The officer plucked it out, holding it up for closer inspection before handing it to the detective. Marco continued his confession, each word incriminating him further. "I was in charge of sales, courting high-end clients purchasing 'exclusive art experiences.' In reality, they were just paying extra for the hidden product."

"So all those 'private viewings' were just a front?" Alan's voice was strained, his knuckles white as he gripped the edge of a nearby crate. Betrayal etched deep lines into his face, making him look far older than his years.

"Exactly. I'd casually mention which pieces contained the latest shipments, all under the guise of discussing the art."

Poor Alan. Her chest ached for her friend, watching his family legacy unravel thread by thread. Greer's eyes landed on a painting in the corner— one she'd admired last week. She shuddered, realizing its pristine beauty had disguised poison. How many others had slipped through unnoticed?

She'd seen enough corruption in her corporate life to recognize the signs, but she'd missed them right here at home.

As the confession dragged on, Marco laid bare a scheme so audacious that Greer's head spun. The comforting scent of wood shavings and oil paint now felt tainted, depravity seeping into every corner of the gallery. With each wild tale implicating Xavier and Jasper, the knot in Greer's chest tightened.

Officers pulled tightly sealed cocaine packets from hidden compartments in the shipping crates, the evidence piling up. Greer glanced at Alan, his shoulders slumped, his face crumpling in distress. She recognized the devastation of a man watching his life's work, his family's legacy, violated by the drugs concealed within.

Her heart broke as Alan's gallery—his home— became a crime scene. The urge to shield him from this twisted mess clawed at her chest, even though she knew it was too late for protection.

If not for the art thefts and the brutal attack on Alan—the bruises on his body still hadn't fully faded—the drugs would have remained undetected, the false crate bottoms blending seamlessly with the packing materials. The minuscule weight discrepancies had gone unnoticed.

The familiar buzz of anxiety hummed beneath her skin as some of the strange happenings made more sense. All those late-night shipments, the peculiar scheduling changes, the way Marco always insisted on personally handling certain deliveries. She should have noticed sooner. Should have pushed harder when things didn't add up.

"I still can't believe we caught him," Greer murmured to Alan as they watched Marco being led away in cuffs, her voice trembling slightly.

Alan gave her shoulder a gentle squeeze, a familiar gesture of comfort. "We make a solid team. Though I gotta say, I'm a little bummed our grand deception didn't get more fanfare." He tried to keep his tone light, but Greer could hear the pain beneath his words.

The bitter taste of betrayal coated her tongue. Marco had been more than an employee—he'd been family to Alan. Now he'd corrupted everything he'd touched with his lies. Her fingers curled into fists at her sides. The journalist in her itched to document every sordid detail, while the friend in her wanted to erase the whole nightmare.

Despite everything, a chuckle escaped Greer's lips, the sound rough and jagged in her throat. "Seriously? After all this, that's what you're hung up on?"

Alan shrugged, a ghost of a smile on his face. "What can I say? I'm a sucker for a good plot twist."

She forced herself to breathe through the tightness in her chest. Trust Alan to find levity in chaos. Maybe that's why they'd clicked from day one—his ability to laugh in the darkness balanced her tendency to overthink every shadow.

She leaned into him slightly, drawing strength from his solid presence as they watched their world unravel. One shocking revelation at a time.

Detective Burman ambled over, the polished floorboards creaking beneath his bulky frame. He leaned in close, his gravelly voice barely above a whisper. "Based on Marco's confession, we've got enough to secure warrants for Jasper Hamel and Xavier Delacroix."

Alan clasped the detective's hand in a firm shake. "Appreciate it, Kyle. Keep us in the loop." He watched Burman exit the gallery, the lingering odor of sweat and fingerprint powder hanging in the air.

Victories never came without strings attached. The spurt of adrenaline mingled with the disillusionment of lost trust. She was keen enough to know when someone was holding back crucial details.

As the adrenaline ebbed, a bittersweet cocktail of victory and apprehension settled deep in Greer's bones. They may have cracked one case, but Marco's disjointed ramblings hinted at a far more sinister puzzle left to solve. Her gaze met Alan's across the room, that familiar spark of tenacity burning bright—the same fire that had initially ignited their partnership all those weeks ago.

Alan quirked an eyebrow, a half-hearted attempt at his usual charming smile. "So, partner, ready to tackle our next thrilling escapade?"

Despite the knots in her stomach, Greer returned the grin. "With you by my side? Always." She straightened her shoulders, her renewed sense of purpose acting as a shield against the doubts nibbling at the edges of her mind.

This wasn't like investigating corrupt tourist traps or exposing overpriced resorts, something she'd hoped to work up to one day. The stakes felt astronomical, threatening to suffocate her with their magnitude. Yet something magnetic pulled her deeper into this mess.

Greer prowled the storeroom, eyes on the mess. "Something about Marco's story stinks," she said, tension pulling at her scalp as she ran a hand through her hair.

Alan glanced up from the scattered paperwork littering the desk. The dim overhead light cast harsh shadows across his furrowed brow. "What's got your gumshoe senses tingling, love?"

Facts used to be her shield, research her blade— but Marco's story slipped through like smoke. This wasn't just muddy—it was rigged.

"His confession was too clean, too rehearsed." The pen Greer held clicked against her fingers in a relentless rhythm, an audible manifestation of her racing thoughts. "Like he was reciting lines from a script."

"And it conveniently glossed over the art heists," Alan added, his fingers absently sliding over the yellowing bruise on his jawline—a painful reminder of the attack that still haunted them both.

The memory of finding Alan that night sent a chill through her. Nothing in her life compared to the horror of seeing him unconscious on the ground, broken and bleeding.

"Not to mention that you ended up beaten almost to death in that alley." Greer's voice caught slightly as their eyes locked, a silent acknowledgment of the unresolved trauma binding them together. An icy tendril of fear snaked down her spine, the unshakable feeling that they were teetering on the precipice of something dark and dangerous. Just how deep did the rot in the art world go, and what twisted revelations awaited them?

TWENTY-TWO

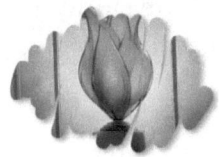

"Shut the front door! Alan, she's dead."

Greer's fingers shook as she laid the faded newspaper clipping on the antique mahogany desk.

"Who, love?" Alan asked.

"Cruella DeVille, of course…"

Greer's past career working in corporate security had taught her to trust her gut, and right now it screamed that this was the breakthrough she'd been waiting for. Her mouth turned to cotton. The desk lamp's soft glow cast an eerie light over the small room, making the old photograph appear even more unsettling.

Alan rushed to look over her shoulder, his typically fluid movements tinged with a hidden tension.

The Art Deco rings adorning his fingers today rattled against the desk as he braced himself—those rings, Greer realized, were his shield against the unknown. Just like her travel assignments were hers. At least on the road, mysteries had logical explanations. Cultural differences. Language barriers. Not whatever this was morphing into.

"Sweetheart, that can't be right. We just saw Vivian at an art show last week." His voice wavered slightly on the word "can't."

"That's the point." Greer tapped the newspaper clipping with her finger: March 15, 2004. The date burned into her memory like coordinates on a map she couldn't quite navigate. "So either Vivian's a ghost… or she staged her own death."

Alan picked up the clipping and read. "This is about a Pamela Bondey, not Vivian Sinclair. And the article—it's just a vague 'reported missing presumed dead' while working in a gallery in Milan. Apparently, there was a major art heist the day she disappeared."

"Look at the photograph, Alan. It's Vivian Sinclair, alright. A little younger, a little thinner. But, I'm telling you it's her." She reached for her phone but stopped. What would she even search? Impersonating the dead? Gallery hauntings? None of it made sense—and that made it all the more urgent to solve.

Alan collapsed into his leather chair, unusually ashen under his flawless tan. His fingers unconsciously fiddled with the ring on his thumb—an anxious tic she recognized.

"A dead ringer for sure. No pun intended... I wonder why my dad kept that article. I assume he must have known her well. Thinking back, my father must have suspected she'd vanished into the shadows rather than face prison. He used to have a saying: 'Some people don't die, they reinvent themselves.' Looks like he was right. I always assumed he was talking about the Nazis who disappeared with so much of the missing art. I certainly never expected it was about someone he might have known himself."

Greer twisted her chestnut curls into a quick bun, stalling as she observed Alan's face crumple under the burden of distrust. If only she could research this the way she did one of her articles. Interview the locals, immerse herself in the culture, and find the thread that connected it all. Three invaluable works gone in six months, each more precious than the last. Now a dead woman roaming the art world? It was too unbelievable, but the sleuth in her thrilled at the chance of truth.

"I've heard whispers of a mysterious player in Hong Kong, Geneva, even Paris. Always attached to a missing piece, always just out of reach. I thought it was a coincidence until now. Like they were pinning it on a boogeyman."

Outside, cable cars rattled up the hill as tourists clustered against the morning mist. The noise was a stark reminder of how isolated they were in this mystery.

"Alan," she said softly, her tone uncharacteristically tender. "I think we need to start digging into your gallery's history. Beginning with everyone who could access the security codes."

The truth cut sharply. She'd shattered people before with what they weren't ready to hear. This time, it was Alan.

Alan's face darkened, a flicker of vulnerability in his eyes. "Even Vincent and Marco?"

Of course, it would come down to the exes. She itched to open her laptop, dig through every ex's past. But this wasn't research—it was personal. Alan didn't need a bulldozer. He needed her.

"Especially them," Greer said, giving his hand a

reassuring squeeze. She felt him tremble slightly at her touch, and her heart ached, knowing the pain it caused him to suspect his former flames. "We can't leave any stone unturned if we want to catch these bastards."

Give her a jungle, a ruin, a stranger's story—anything but this. Now she was neck-deep in feelings and suspects with no exit plan.

Alan nodded grimly as thunder rumbled in the distance, his jaw clenched tight. "Buckle up, darling. You're about to get a crash course in the sordid underbelly of the art world. But be warned, some secrets are best left in the dark."

Her curiosity sparked like lightning at those words. The promise of uncovering hidden truths sent a familiar thrill through her veins, even as guilt gnawed at her conscience for finding excitement in Alan's predicament.

Greer's stomach churned with a mix of icy dread and electric anticipation. Like a detective matching up fragments of ancient pottery, she couldn't resist investigating further, even when common sense screamed at her to back away. In her experience, those were precisely the secrets worth dragging into the light, regardless of the consequences. The irony wasn't lost on her that the biggest thrill of her career was unfolding in her own backyard, not some exotic, far-off land.

———

THE FOLLOWING WEEK, THEY SET ANOTHER TRAP. Her mental notepad kicked into overdrive, methodically reviewing each detail of their plan. The insatiable need for answers in her couldn't help but catalog this moment. Greer hauled a bulky suitcase down the gallery steps, projecting her voice despite her pounding heart.

"Alan, get a move on! We'll miss the plane!"

Alan emerged a moment later, his breezy demeanor betrayed only by the faint circles under his eyes.

"On my way, love! You know I had to agonize over the perfect travel ascot!"

Climbing into their getaway cab, Greer spied a shadowy figure observing from across the road. Her social anxiety had her twitchy about the attention they were drawing. This wasn't like observing things from a safe distance—she was the story now. Primal fear warred with the heady rush of the chase, but she kept her face a mask of calm. The lure was cast.

They had a nice dinner at a little Indian restaurant down the street from the airport, keeping to their ploy. After killing a couple of hours away from the city, they caught a new cab and returned to the gallery under the cloak of darkness. Her independence had always been her shield, but now she found herself oddly grateful for Alan's presence. Not that she'd admit it—maintaining professional distance was practically her superpower. Greer's clammy hand gripped Alan's, the chill of his rings biting into her skin.

"Not a sound once we're inside," she breathed.

Alan gave a curt nod, his normally mirthful expression grave and determined, tinged with fear.

They settled in for the tense night ahead, hearts pounding as they waited to see who might emerge from the shadows. This was nothing like researching ancient temples or interviewing local artisans. No amount of cultural sensitivity training had prepared her for amateur detective work. Greer took a deep breath, trying to calm her racing thoughts, but her mind buzzed with a dizzying array of possibilities, each more thrilling than the last.

In the darkness, Greer sat frozen, her clammy hands clutching her phone as she fixated on the gallery wall. Why was she unable to resist the pull of another mystery? An unfamiliar cocktail of exhilaration and dread tightened her chest, a feeling that had been her constant companion since she'd arrived in San Francisco. With shaky hands, she typed her notes into her phone, based on her memory of the details listed in the files Alan had given her to review, connecting the missing pieces to Alan's old flames.

"Ivory carving gone February 20th when Vincent was on security," she mumbled, fingers flying across the screen. Her grip tightened around the phone. Her instincts rarely steered her wrong.

"Then in mid-May, there was the missing blown glass vase from Ireland that you said disappeared, but were told it had been broken... And that rare Hiroshige print vanished July 2nd, right after Phil's abrupt exit. None priceless enough to cause a stir, but still worth enough to matter."

Her vision blurred as a seed of doubt took root. The thrill of uncovering hidden truths mingled with an unsettling awareness that she might be pulling at threads better left alone. The rational part of her brain insisted on examining every angle, every possibility, while her gut screamed that she was onto something significant. What if her hunch was wrong? What if she were leading them straight into the lion's den?

Greer's forehead creased as a troubling thought hit her. Trust came at a premium in her world. Now here she was, potentially uncovering a level of deception she'd never fathomed. Were all these heists tied to Alan's trusted inner circle? The idea made her insides twist into knots. Disloyalty always cuts the deepest.

TWENTY-THREE

Hushed voices floated down the gallery hall. Greer's heart nearly leapt out of her chest, and Alan went rigid beside her.

This was definitely trouble. In the gloom, his hand found hers, a wordless lifeline that grounded her spiraling thoughts. Straining to hear, she checked the recorder with bated breath.

"...the Asawa sculpture's next," a rough voice growled. "Boss has a customer already lined up."

"And Caputo's clueless?" A second voice probed.

Everything made sense with nauseating clarity. All those little inconsistencies she'd noticed around the gallery, the misplaced artifacts, the odd hours kept by certain staff members—she knew there was far more going on even after learning about Marco's confession. Greer's eyes nearly popped out of her skull. She glanced at Alan, watching the blood drain from his face. Even in the faint light, she could see the gut-wrenching betrayal written all over his features.

"Nope," the first voice snickered. "Him and his nosy novelist pal are too busy playing detective, chasing after drug pushers. Where'd they head off to this weekend, anyway?"

"Paris, from what I overheard. The timing couldn't be better."

Her head pounded. She'd insisted on this stake-out, convinced Alan to trust her gut feeling. Now here they were, huddled in darkness while criminals plotted to rob the gallery again. Greer's hands trembled as she fiddled with the recording device, a cold sweat trickling down her spine. Their plan had worked, but the victory felt hollow. Burman's dismissive attitude towards their theory stung like a slap in the face, leaving them exposed and alone in this dangerous game.

"Alan," her voice barely squeezing through her tight throat, "those voices… do they sound familiar to you?"

He shook his head, his grip on her hand tightening. "No, but they sure know who I am," he breathed back, his tone laced with unease.

As the mysterious figures moved towards the gallery entrance, their voices fading, Greer's mind spun with terrifying possibilities. Who was this shadowy boss? The question hung in the air, pressing against her chest like a physical weight. Pushing past the percolating terror, she focused on memorizing every detail with desperate precision. This was exactly why she preferred writing about places. They rarely involved people who skulked around in darkness.

Suddenly, the sharp click of expensive shoes on the polished floor echoed through the gallery, making Greer's heart skip a beat.

"You got what I asked for?" a new voice demanded. The voice came with a click of a lighter.

She pressed herself flatter against the wall, cursing her inability to blend into shadows like the seasoned investigative reporters she'd always watched in movies. Travel writing had taught her many things, but stealth operations weren't covered in the employee handbook.

"Yes, sir," came the mumbled reply.

"Good. Let's get out of here."

Alan's fingers dug into Greer's palm with sudden urgency. "Son of a beach! It's Dominic Vancetti," he hissed, his voice barely audible.

The name sliced through her thoughts like a knife. Of course, it would be Dominic, the man who'd been circling the Bayside Art Collective like a vulture eyeing its next meal. She barely recalled meeting him the night of the Riviera show. His presence here was no coincidence, and the realization made her head spin. Apparently, her life had transformed from a pleasant travel column into some twisted crime noir, complete with shadowy figures and cryptic conversations. Yet, this was something far more sinister.

In the darkness, they locked eyes. The panic in Alan's gaze mirrored her own, and Greer's pulse pounded in her ears, the adrenaline making her hands shake despite Alan's steadying grip.

As the front door slammed shut, the lock clicked into place, and Greer let out a shaky breath she didn't realize she'd been holding. The intruders were gone, but the questions they left behind weighed heavily on her shoulders. Just how many secrets was the gallery hiding?

"Alan," Greer whispered, her voice quivering with a mix of fear and determination. "This is serious. Are you sure you want to keep digging?" She searched his face in the dim light, knowing she'd follow him into the fire, but hating herself for the blind loyalty.

The familiar tightness seized her chest. Her entire career had been built on calculated risks and meticulous research, not stumbling through darkened galleries playing amateur detective. And yet here she stood, ready to throw logic aside for a friend.

Emerging from their hiding spot, Greer and Alan hurried back to the main gallery, their footsteps echoing in the eerie silence. Alan's grip on Greer's hand was firm, but she could feel the slight tremor in his fingers. "We can't turn back now, Greer," he said, his voice low and resolute. "This is my family's legacy we're talking about. We've got to stop them."

Her throat constricted. But Alan had become family—the kind that actually mattered, not the sort that demanded conformity over Sunday dinners.

Greer squeezed his hand in return, a silent promise of support. The investigation settled heavily on her shoulders, a burden she hadn't expected to bear. Somewhere along the way, her professional detachment had vanished, leaving her emotionally invested in a way that both thrilled and terrified her.

This wasn't like documenting indigenous crafts or reviewing five-star resorts. Those situations had clear boundaries, neat endings. But now? She'd crossed an invisible line between observer and participant.

"Let's head upstairs," she managed, hating the waver in her voice that betrayed her unease.

Alan's hand tightened around hers as they navigated the shadowy gallery, the musty air thick with secrets and hidden dangers. Greer's mind raced, trying to fit Dominic's involvement into the tangled web of clues. The idea sent a chill down her spine, but she clung to her determination, refusing to let fear gain the upper hand.

As they wove through the gallery's dim recesses, Greer's senses were on high alert. The pounding of her heart seemed to echo in her ears, a constant reminder of the perilous game they were playing. And she couldn't exactly fact-check her way out of it. The smooth silk of Alan's shirt brushed against her arm, a small comfort amidst the adrenaline coursing through her veins.

She froze. "Alan," she hissed urgently, her face

searching his in the darkness, "do you think Dominic Vancetti is the one behind all this?"

She'd asked countless questions before, but none of those conversations had ever felt this loaded with tension. She had no doubt they were onto something massive. Something that could make her previous investigations look like tourist fluff pieces.

Their gazes locked, a silent understanding passing between them. They had ventured too far to turn back now, the point of no return left in the dust of their relentless pursuit of the truth.

Alan's expression hardened, his jaw clenched with grim determination. "It would explain why he's been sniffing around the gallery lately," he murmured, his tone laced with tension. He reached for her hand once more, his grip steady and reassuring, a lifeline in the chaos.

Her fingers tingled where they touched his—not from romance, but from pure nerves. Of course, this would be her experience in a big city like San Francisco. She read about dangers like this in other places, in distant locations. She'd been naïve to not expect it here.

They finally reached the door, Greer's fingers shaking slightly as she fumbled with the handle. The stale air rushed to greet them as they stumbled into the narrow stairwell, the dim light casting eerie shadows on the walls.

With trembling hands, Greer locked the door behind them, her breath coming in short, ragged gasps as she leaned heavily against the handrail. If her mother could see her now. Beside her, Alan ran a hand through his tousled hair, his usually impeccable appearance disheveled and worn.

In Alan's eyes, Greer saw a reflection of her own swirling emotions. The thrill of the chase, tempered by a growing sense of unease. Somewhere along the way, their partnership had evolved into something deeper, something that made her heart clench with a fierce desire to keep him safe.

The familiar ache of caring too much crept in. It was easier to keep moving, keep running, than admit how much she needed someone watching her back.

"Galloping gremlins, that was close," Greer managed.

Alan's lips tightened into a grim line, his usual carefree grin notably absent. "Too bloody close. But we're making progress, darling. One step at a time."

Progress. Right. Because nearly getting caught was totally part of the plan. She should be sitting at a desk, chasing down reviews of a local eatery, not playing amateur detective.

A wave of gratitude washed over Greer. "You're right. We've got this."

"Darn straight we do," Alan agreed, a flicker of his trademark smile returning. "So, what's our next brilliant move, Detective Caldwell?"

The nickname should have irritated her—she wrote travel pieces for heaven's sake, not crime reports. Yet something about this mess felt oddly right, like finding an unmarked trail that led to the perfect vista.

"I need wine," she said.

"I'm thinking a martini would soothe these nerves." He shrugged.

She grinned as they shoved off the banister and climbed up to the apartment. Each creak of the wooden steps beneath their feet a harsh reminder of the danger that lurked. Greer shut and locked the second door behind her as a precaution. The more locked doors between them and Dominic Vancetti's goons, the better.

Dropping onto the couch, she slipped off her shoes, rested her head against the back, and closed her eyes. She focused on her breathing while Alan puttered in the kitchen.

Greer's mind battled with a dizzying array of possibilities and connections threatening to over-whelm her.

"Here you go, darling. A dirty drink for a dirty mess."

With a grin, she stood and accepted the cloudy beverage. Martinis in hand, they retreated to the window seat in the darkened living room, the city's fog-shrouded streets mirroring the hazy uncertainty of their predicament. She pressed her forehead against the cool glass, desperate for a moment of clarity.

Facts. She needed facts. Not hunches or half-formed theories. The kind of solid details she'd stake her reputation on. This wasn't some story about boutique hotels—lives hung in the balance.

"Alan, this goes way beyond stolen art or even drugs. There's a bigger game afoot here."

Alan's shoulder brushed against hers, a solid, comforting presence. "I know. We're in deep, darling. But whatever comes, we're in it together."

Together. The word sparked equal parts comfort and panic. This was not what she was comfortable with. She preferred keeping the world at a safe distance. Now here she was, tangled up in a conspiracy with her flamboyant roommate of all people.

Greer's brain shifted into high gear. "That conversation we overheard ties into the thefts. The real question is, who's pulling the strings?"

"Well, I can certainly tell you, Dominic, Xavier, and Marco aren't exactly criminal masterminds, in my opinion."

Alan leaned into her, giving her shoulder a gentle squeeze. She could feel the faint tremor in his touch, a subtle tell that brought a lump to her throat. It was the thinnest of cracks in his meticulously crafted facade.

Instinct screamed for space. But Alan deserved more than her walls. Not now. Not when the ground beneath him was already cracking.

The once vibrant living room felt suffocating, the shadows dancing ominously on the walls. Even the comforting aroma of Alan's signature aromatherapy blend had turned stale and uninviting, a harsh reminder of how quickly their optimism had soured.

Greer immediately pulled out her notebook, her fingers white-knuckled around the pen. "Okay, let's break this down," she said, fighting the urge to run

—running was safer, always had been. "What exactly did we hear?"

Facts. Data. Analysis. This was her territory. She could dissect this situation, piece by piece, like one of her articles, until the truth emerged. If only her hands would stop shaking long enough to write properly.

Alan sucked in a breath, his perfectly manicured nails digging into his palm. "They mentioned a boss. That means these were just the hired thugs. If we continue the premise that Dominic is not the mastermind, I have no idea where we start…" He attempted a weak laugh. "Though God knows his fashion choices are criminal enough."

The forced levity in his voice made her chest ache. How many times had she relied on the same defense mechanism during her assignments? Deflect, deflect, deflect—until the truth became manageable.

"Yes!" Greer exclaimed, scribbling furiously, grateful for the momentary lightness. "And something about a 'big score' coming up. Alan, I think they're planning a heist." Her heart hammered against her ribs, each beat a reminder of how much she had to lose if she got this wrong.

Something about all of this was just not making

sense, no matter which way she looked at it. She couldn't really see how the drugs and thefts were connected. Drug smuggling was one thing. But this? This felt different.

Alan's face paled, the usually rosy cheeks now ashen. "Here?"

The raw fear in his voice stripped away her last defenses. She couldn't maintain a professional distance, not with Alan. Not when his gallery meant everything to him.

Greer bit her lip, her brow furrowed in concentration. The metallic taste of blood surprised her—she hadn't realized how hard she'd been biting. "It's possible. We need to cross-reference everything we've learned. There must be a pattern we're missing."

TWENTY-FOUR

As they sat there in the silence, the weight of the situation settled over them like a heavy blanket. Greer felt a growing sense of danger.

"Alan," she said, looking up at her friend, her voice barely above a whisper, "are you sure about this?"

The question hung between them, and Greer fought the urge to take it back, to shoulder this burden alone like she always did. Safer that way.

Alan met her gaze, his voice filled with determination, though his fingers nervously twisted the rings he often wore—armor disguised as accessories.

"Absolutely, darling. No one steals from Alan Caputo and gets away with it."

A familiar ache bloomed in her chest. Alan's loyalty, his fierce determination, reminded her too much of herself before Peter had stripped away her naïve faith in people. She should walk away. She knew better now. And yet...

Greer nodded, feeling a surge of admiration for Alan's passion, even as her stomach knotted with the familiar fear of getting too close.

"Then we keep going. But we need to be smarter. No more close calls like tonight."

The words tasted like ash in her mouth. How many times had she promised herself 'never again'? But here she was, diving headfirst into another potential catastrophe. Because apparently, she never learned.

As they prepared for the next phase of their investigation, Greer couldn't help but feel they were standing on the precipice of something much bigger. Her hands trembled slightly as she arranged the papers. The same way they had the night she'd discovered her husband's plans to leave her, a memory that tightened her throat.

The past and present blurred together, a nause-ating spiral of déjà vu. She wished she were halfway to the airport by now, booking a flight to some remote destination where complicated friendships and unsolved mysteries couldn't follow. Instead, her feet remained planted firmly on Alan's vintage Persian rug, her stubborn loyalty winning out over self-preservation. Again.

Greer whipped out her trusty notebook, her knuckles turning white as she gripped the pen like a lifeline.

"Alright, let's dissect this mess." Greer chewed on her lower lip, her brow knitted in deep thought. "What juicy tidbits did we overhear?"

As they scrutinized their notes and clues, the gravity of their predicament settled over them like a suffocating fog. Greer felt the telltale buzz of anticipation, but a creeping sense of foreboding undercut it.

"Alan," she murmured, a hint of excitement lacing her voice, "I think I've found a link between those shady conversations we overheard and your ex, Vincent."

Alan's eyebrows shot up, his gaudy rings glinting in the lamplight as he gestured for her to continue. "Well, well, do tell, darling. What's that conniving ex of mine gotten himself mixed up in this time?"

Greer's lips twitched into a wry half-smile. "You

remember how those goons mentioned an 'inside man' during our little stakeout? Turns out, according to these old gallery records, Vincent had full access to the gallery while you two were an item. And get this, the timing of your messy breakup…"

"…lines up perfectly with the last theft," Alan finished, his voice catching slightly. He looked away, blinking back the sting of betrayal. "The night he walked out, he asked me to meet him in the gallery. I'm such a fool. I actually believed we had a solid relationship."

Her heart broke. She knew all too well how love could blind you to the obvious. How many times had she ignored red flags in her own relationship, choosing to believe the comfortable lie?

She reached out, giving his hand a comforting squeeze. "Hey, don't be so hard on yourself. Hindsight's always 20/20."

A bitter smile played on his lips, but the pain still lingered in his eyes. "Who'd have thought my train wreck of a love life would lead to all this cloak-and-dagger nonsense? It's like we've stumbled into some half-baked pulp novel gone awry."

She'd experienced it herself not that long ago, but nothing had prepared her for watching her best friend's heart shatter in real time. Facts and research she could handle. Emotions? Those were definitely not in her skill set.

As they continued to consider each note, Greer marveled at how effortlessly they worked in tandem. Her razor-sharp inquisitiveness complemented Alan's intimate knowledge of the gallery's inner workings, forming a formidable investigative duo. But that very closeness set off alarm bells in her head.

The urge to bolt clawed at her chest. She'd perfected the art of keeping relationships superficial. Quick hellos over coffee, emotionless nods at events. Safe. Controlled. But here she was, actually seeking company. When had that happened?

"You know," she said softly, absently tracing the recently bare ring finger. "I've always been good at keeping people at a safe distance. After Peter... I swore I'd never let myself trust anyone that deeply again. But this... working with you... feels different somehow."

The truth lodged like a stone. Letting someone in was dangerous. But somehow, Alan had slipped past every defense before she could stop him.

Alan's gaze softened, and he reached across the table to still her restless hands. "Greer, my dear, you may be a globetrotter with a trail of broken hearts in your wake, but sometimes the most exhilarating adventures are the ones we embark on with a trusted partner by our side. Even the ones that scare the bejeebus out of us."

Her eyes pooled, and she chuckled. The only broken heart was hers.

As they put the finishing touches on their game plan, Greer marveled at the unexpected path that had led them here. What began as an uneasy alliance between mismatched roommates had blossomed into a partnership forged in the fires of danger and discovery. And if she were honest with herself, the depth of that bond was what terrified her most.

TWENTY-FIVE

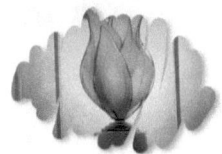

G reer strode into the gallery the next morning, juggling her laptop and an oversized thermos of Irish Breakfast Tea. As she set her things down, the gravity of their investigation weighed heavily on her. Another day of playing amateur detective while pretending to maintain a professional distance. At least she'd achieved the appearance of looking composed while internally spiraling. She hoped anyway. The caffeine was a necessity, but her stomach rebelled at the thought of coffee, her nerves already frayed from the constant tightrope walk between observer and participant. Her mother's warning echoed in her mind, *curiosity killed the cat*, and it could bury a journalist just as easily.

Alan was hunched over a pile of musty ledgers, his signature silk button-up replaced by a no-nonsense black turtleneck sweater.

The sight of Alan in anything but his typical flamboyant attire sent a fresh wave of anxiety through her system. When even he dropped his carefully maintained persona, something was definitely amiss.

"Well, don't you look uncharacteristically sensible today," Greer quipped, depositing a chocolate croissant on his desk, the familiar back-and-forth providing a welcome distraction from her mounting unease.

"Darling, I'll have you know that black is the epitome of sophistication," Alan retorted, sliding a weathered leather-bound book her way. "Even I recognize when it's time to get down to brass tacks. Take a gander at this. These are gallery records from 2004."

Greer's fingers hovered above the cracked spine. That year again. Everything kept circling back— like someone had bookmarked history and was flipping back through the pages, erasing what didn't belong. Her fingers itched to grab the book, that familiar scholarly excitement warring with her instinct for self-preservation.

Settling into the corner chair, Greer balanced the hefty ledger on her knees. Normally, the comforting aroma of aged paper would soothe her frazzled nerves, but today, it only served as a stark reminder of this investigation and had left an indelible mark on her psyche. But when had she ever chosen the sensible path?

"I had no idea she worked for your father," Greer mused, tapping an entry with her finger. "Look here, Vivian Sinclair's inaugural acquisition for the gallery. Lot 256: A very large and fine 19th-century Chinese carved Ivory Bridge Group."

Alan's face clouded over. "That was the first piece to vanish on my watch. Losing something so valuable was a real kick in the teeth."

"The staccato click of high heels on hardwood interrupted Greer's response. They whirled around to find a stunning blonde standing in the doorway —Vivian Sinclair, very much alive.

Greer's stomach dropped. "You're supposed to be dead." She blurted.

Vivian smirked. "Darling, you can't believe everything you read in the papers. That little obituary was... a necessary fiction."

A chill rippled through her chest. The woman's

presence here couldn't be coincidence—nothing in her experience ever was.

"I hope I'm not intruding," the woman purred, her smile a touch too flawless. "I have a meeting scheduled with Mr. Caputo regarding next month's auction."

Alan shot Greer a look of panic. With everything happening, they'd both forgotten all about the meeting. She gave his shoulder a reassuring squeeze, projecting an air of composure she didn't quite feel. Her heart skipped a beat, and the familiar rush of adrenaline sparked through her veins.

"Not a problem at all," Greer said breezily, gathering her things despite the numbness in her fingers. "I was on my way out, anyway."

As she brushed past the blonde, Greer feigned a stumble, grabbing the woman's designer bag to steady herself. "Oh my gosh, I'm such a klutz! Forgive me."

The woman's perfume clung too long in the air —musky, familiar. Greer blinked. She'd smelled it weeks ago in Alan's apartment. Her pulse skipped. This wasn't a coincidence.

The woman's smile remained fixed, but her eyes flashed with a predatory glint. "No worries, it happens."

Greer suppressed a shudder, realizing she'd just painted a target on her own back. This woman was no mere impersonator. She was a hunter.

The thrum of danger pulsed through her body, sharp and electric. Ducking into an alcove outside Alan's office, Greer pressed her back against the cool wall, trying to calm her racing pulse. Every instinct screamed at her that this wasn't her battle to fight.

She risked a glance back at the office, where the faux Vivian was draped over Alan's desk, invading his space. A fierce protectiveness surged through her chest.

Alan was the closest thing to an actual friend she'd had in years. The thought of someone using him as a pawn in their scheme made her hands curl into useless fists. She'd spent her whole life observing from a safe distance, never interfering. Now the story had come home, threatening one of the few people who'd slipped past her carefully cultivated independence.

The fog crept in, shrouding the gallery's glass exterior, blurring the lines between right and wrong. Her mother's voice echoed in her head. "Always running off, never thinking things through." But for her, staying put felt more dangerous than fleeing. It warred within her, torn between self-preservation and the relentless pull of the truth. Priceless art was hidden somewhere in the city, a dead woman's identity stolen, and the situation had spiraled into something sinister.

Greer squared her shoulders, silencing the warning bells in her head that sounded an awful lot like her mother's voice. This wasn't some travel piece she could polish up with clever metaphors and cultural insights. No editor to smooth rough edges, no chance for a rewrite. One wrong move and the consequences wouldn't just fill column inches; they could fill body bags, but there was no turning back now.

The die was cast, and she was all in. Heaven help her.

Vivian didn't stay long. With a glare at Greer, she sashayed out of the gallery as if she didn't have a care in the world.

Alan followed her out until he reached where Greer was standing.

"Well, that was a colossal waste of time. Then again, most meetings really could be better served as an email." Alan rolled his eyes.

With a shrug, they exchanged a glance.

"She wanted to confirm the Kandinsky was going to be up for sale," he said.

"Seriously strange," Greer said.

CHAPTER
TWENTY-SIX

G reer's shallow breaths echoed through the deserted gallery, intertwining with the gentle pitter-patter of Phoenix's paws. The ginger tabby scampered ahead, his tail raised like a fluffy torch, navigating her through the shadowy space. After a few weeks together, she'd learned to trust his instincts. His comforting presence calmed her pounding heart. It was amusing how a stray cat had become so important to her.

"Where are you taking me, you impish kitty?" Greer muttered, her eyes darting across the art-covered walls. She couldn't help but laugh at herself, following a cat through an art gallery. The paintings appeared to observe her, evoking an unease deep within. Who knew there was such intrigue lurking beneath the surface of the art world, although maybe that's what had lured her in? Perhaps she should have stuck to writing about quaint bed-and-breakfasts instead of chasing leads through darkened galleries. The gritty reality hidden behind glossy veneers resonated with her.

Phoenix halted, glancing back at Greer with an insistent meow.

Her mother would have a field day with this. Her eldest daughter taking direction from a cat while prowling through an art gallery after hours. Add it to the growing list of "unconventional life choices" that made holiday dinners so delightfully awkward. She hastened her stride, her sensible loafers hardly making a sound on the gleaming floor. Her hands quivered faintly. She'd never reveal it, but these late-night explorations petrified her. Yet, fear of the dark trumped fear of failure, of confirming her mother's assertions about her "foolhardy obsession with things better left untouched."

As she turned a corner, she noticed a looming form under a grimy tarp. "What have you discovered, kitty?" Greer whispered, nearing the enigmatic object. The rational part of her brain squawked to turn back, to leave this particular mystery unsolved. But that same stubborn determination now pushed her forward.

The pungent scent of dust tickled Greer's nostrils as she yanked the heavy tarp aside, causing particles to swirl in the glow of her flashlight. Her breath hitched. There, illuminated by the faint light of San Francisco's most esteemed art gallery, rested an ornate Victorian chair. Dark, rust-hued stains spread across its once-opulent upholstery like grotesque blossoms.

"What do you think, Phoenix?" Greer murmured to the ginger tabby. She often pondered if he grasped how much his companionship meant to her, how he kept the suffocating isolation at bay.

Phoenix inspected the chair's ornate leg, his tail flicking warily.

At least cats didn't wax poetic. Their loyalty came without strings attached—unlike humans, who seemed programmed to disappoint.

This was precisely why she'd chosen travel writing—constant motion meant no attachments, no expectations, no chance for history to repeat itself. Yet here she stood, rooted to the spot by a piece of furniture that shouldn't exist. The universe, it seemed, had a twisted sense of humor.

She crouched low to inspect the frame—and

froze. Along the inner leg, carved into the dark wood, was a tiny, almost imperceptible mark: a serpent devouring its tail.

The click of dress shoes on wood startled her, and she whirled around, hands quivering. Alan stepped out from the shadows, his silk shirt shimmering in the faint light. Seeing him elicited a mix of solace and apprehension—the harsh experience had taught her that trust was a fragile thing, easily fractured and arduous to rebuild.

"Darling, you're white as a sheet!" Alan's dramatic inflection betrayed a hint of strain. "What hidden gem have you stumbled upon in our humble abode—wait, what?" His voice faltered as he noticed the chair. "That's… definitely not part of our collection."

The recognizable flutter of unanswered questions filled her gut. Greer knew better than to dismiss her instincts when they cried that something was off.

"Are you certain?" Greer urged, gauging his response. The gallery's muted illumination painted shadows across his features, evoking thoughts of all the instances she believed she truly knew someone, only to unearth their concealed facets. She had learned to interpret the minute fluctuations in

Alan's meticulously crafted demeanor. Presently, behind his nonchalant exterior, she sensed a genuine disquiet that echoed her own.

"To the best of my knowledge, yes," he replied, prowling around the chair, his jewelry glinting as he moved. "Although I can't be entirely sure. This piece… it's in a league of its own."

Greer massaged her forehead, the pressure of recent events squeezing her skull in a relentless grip. "Alan, I think we could use a moment to regroup."

Her companion's posture stiffened. "You may be onto something there." He scanned the shadowy room. "But let's relocate. These walls are a bit too nosy for my liking."

"Shall we go back upstairs?"

Alan's expression brightened. "Capital idea, my dear!"

They climbed the stairs to the apartment, and she dropped onto the couch. Alan bustled into the kitchen, calling over his shoulder, "Get comfy, my dear! I've got a Burgundy calling our names."

Minutes later, he returned with a couple of glasses and a bottle of wine, setting them down with a theatrical flourish. Greer couldn't suppress a smile. Another surreal moment in what had become her distinctly off-kilter life. "When I moved to San

Francisco, I never imagined I'd be wrapped up in something like this."

"Ah, life's full of surprises, isn't it?" Alan popped an olive into his mouth, a mischievous glint in his eye. "So, what really drew you to our enchanting city?"

The familiar urge to deflect rose up, to package her answer in neat, simplistic prose. But something about Alan's genuine interest made her hesitate. Maybe it was the alcohol. Or maybe she was just tired of maintaining that carefully measured distance.

Greer sipped her wine, the warm liquid doing little to soothe the tightness in her throat.

"I was chasing a dream, I suppose. Epic Destinations offered me the chance to write about amazing places, to inspire people to explore the world." She paused, worrying her lower lip between her teeth. The truth hovered there, demanding to be acknowledged. For once, she didn't push it away. "But if I'm being honest, I was really just running away." The admission left a bitter taste in her mouth, conjuring memories of that fateful night—the discarded note, the empty drawers, the realization of how thoroughly she'd been betrayed.

Alan leaned in, his rings clinking softly against his glass. "Running away from what, darling?"

She could write thousand-word articles about just about anything without breaking a sweat, but personal conversations like this made her feel like she was translating a language she barely understood.

"Mostly expectations," Greer sighed, fidgeting with a strand of her chestnut hair, a nervous tic she'd had since childhood. "I had a very different vision of how my life would turn out. San Francisco symbolized freedom to me." The word 'freedom' felt bittersweet on her tongue, a promise she wasn't sure she merited.

"I know that feeling all too well," Alan said, his fingers tracing the rim of his mug. "The gallery's been in my family for generations, but being the unconventional son who wanted to shake things up wasn't always a cakewalk."

TWENTY-SEVEN

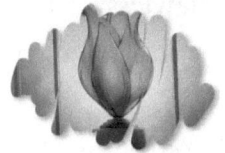

As they continued to open up, Greer felt a rare sense of peace wash over her. The instinct to shield herself from potential pain still lurked at the edges of her mind, but it was less insistent now. The familiar urge to bolt faded with each passing moment, like a tide slowly receding from shore. How strange that she felt safer here, perched on Alan's velvet settee, than she had in ages. Despite her usual guarded nature, she shared more than she had in years. Something about Alan's sincerity and the warmth of his eccentric apartment—the soft glow of antique lamps, the inviting aroma of old books and expensive wine—put her at ease.

"You know," Greer confessed, her fingers interlaced tightly in her lap, "I sometimes wonder if I'll ever find my place in this world."

The words tumbled out before she could stop them. Classic Greer, give her a remote locale, and she navigated it flawlessly. But genuine human connection? That was her personal Bermuda Triangle.

Alan reached out, his hand a comforting warmth on hers. "Greer, darling, home is more than just a location. It's the people who make us feel like we belong."

After everything, could she really risk anchoring herself to another relationship? Even if it was just a friendship? The thought sent a flutter of panic through her chest.

A smile tugged at Greer's lips, gratitude swelling in her chest despite the vulnerability that constricted her throat. "I know you're right, Alan. I've been running for so long, I almost forgot how it feels to genuinely connect with someone."

While she preferred keeping people at arm's length, treating relationships like her travel assignments; observe, document, and move on. Here she sat, actually letting someone new past her carefully crafted defenses.

Leaning closer, Alan's gaze held hers with a

gentle intensity. "Letting people in can be scary, can't it?"

Greer nodded, swallowing hard. "It's absolutely petrifying, but this investigation… it's making me face that fear head-on." The irony wasn't lost on her.

"It's like every time we think we're getting closer to the truth, we run into another dead end. We're just grasping at straws here!"

"I get it, I really do!" Alan insisted, his usual effervescence dampened by concern. "But we can't throw in the towel now. Someone's focused on ruining the gallery. The attack on me, the break-ins, the thefts… it's all linked. And I've got a hunch Vivian Sinclair is involved, but I can't nail her without proof."

Alan's gallery represented more than just art—it was his legacy, his passion. And here she was, caught up in another mess that challenged her carefully cultivated independence. Yet something about this pulled at her analytical nature, demanding answers.

Greer set her wineglass down, a steely resolve settling over her. "Then let's get that proof. We need a solid strategy."

She opened her laptop and pulled up the

gallery's blueprints. "If they know the layout better than we do, we're already behind." Her voice was low, even. Focused.

"We need to think like criminals. Not curators."

That's precisely why, two nights later, Greer found herself once again hiding in the gallery, tucked in behind an imposing abstract sculpture, her heart pounding so hard she feared it might burst from her chest. Each breath felt deafening in the shadowy gallery, reverberating like thunder in her ears. Her muscles screamed from staying motionless, icy sweat trickling down her back. Nearby, concealed behind their meticulously positioned bait—the centerpiece of the forthcoming exhibition—Alan's breathing grew ragged with anticipation.

THE LAST RAYS OF SUNLIGHT FADED FROM THE gallery windows, plunging the gallery into an eerie twilight. Greer felt a shiver run down her spine, her sight straining to adjust to the growing darkness. Her fingertips tingled with adrenaline as she pressed them against the cool floor, grounding herself in the moment. Earlier clues had pointed to a shadowy figure—an unfamiliar series of shipping manifests, whispered conversations between Marco and Jasper —but that had turned out to be a drug smuggling operation not tied to the rest of the problems the gallery faced. This new danger was tangible, as real as the fear coating her tongue like metal.

Around midnight, a soft scraping sound made her freeze. Someone was coming in through the front door. Her throat constricted, and she forced herself to take shallow, silent breaths through her nose. Whoever was entering had a new key, limiting the suspects but amplifying the motives. Footsteps crept past the decoy artifact they'd set out, heading toward the storage room instead.

"Greer?" Alan's whisper cut through the darkness. "Did you hear that?"

Her stomach lurched. When had her life turned into this bizarre fusion of Nancy Drew meets Instagram influencer?

She held up a finger, listening intently. The cold marble floor beneath her seeped through her clothes, a reminder of how exposed they were, how amateur this whole operation was.

She should not be hiding in the dark like some wannabe vigilante. But her dear friend needed her help, and loyalty—her perpetual weakness—had dragged her into this mess. At least her writing had taught her how to stay perfectly still while photographing wildlife. Usually, though, the wildlife wasn't carrying keys to the gallery. *Why couldn't the detective take them seriously? He was so convinced everything had been solved with the arrest of Marco. Even after Alan had told them about Dominic Vancetti.* They were dangling in the wind right now because of it.

The security system's chirp cut through the silence, then fell quiet. Whoever their intruder was, they knew the updated code. The familiar scent of oil paint and wood polish suddenly felt oppressive, suffocating, like the weight of her choices pressing down on her chest.

This was it. The moment they'd been waiting for. So why did this feel so much more personal, so much more dangerous? Perhaps because this time, she couldn't just hop on a plane and escape when things got complicated. The moment she'd been running toward—or maybe running from.

"Get ready," she breathed, her fingers trembling as they tightened around the small flashlight in her hand.

The tension in the air was palpable as they waited, poised for action. Greer couldn't help but reflect on how her life had led her to this moment. Her eyes closed tight as she processed the absurdity.

Perfect. At least her next article would be interesting, assuming she was still around to actually write it. What did it say about her that she'd found herself only after losing everything else?

A shadowy figure crept through the darkness. The sound of metal tools scraping against the display case lock sending Greer's heart into overdrive. She fought to steady her rapid, shallow breaths as she watched the intruder hunch over and focus on their task. This was it—the moment of truth.

Alan caught her eye, mouthing a single word. "Now?"

A hysterical laugh threatened to bubble up in her throat. Here she was, hiding in the shadows with her flamboyant roommate, playing cat-and-mouse with a criminal. Her mother would have an aneurysm if she knew. Then again, her mother still thought she was wasting her life by not looking for another husband and settling down in the suburbs with 2.5 kids and a minivan. Like that was ever going to happen. Minivan's ewe!

Greer's palms were slick with sweat, her pulse pounding so fiercely she was certain the intruder could hear it echoing through the gallery. But it wasn't just the danger that terrified her. It was the desperate need for this moment to validate the risks they'd taken.

She counted down each second thick with dread.

Darkness pressed in, their trap set.

If it failed, everything crumbled.

TWENTY-EIGHT

G reer's eyes widened as Alan silently nodded towards Dominic, who moved with dangerous precision towards the priceless artifact. Her nerves kicked into overdrive, tingling with the thrill of catching a thief red-handed.

Alan's harsh whisper cut through the tense silence, pointing out a glinting object in Dominic's grasp. Greer's focus shifted swiftly, capturing the incriminating evidence without hesitation. The room pulsed with anticipation as they awaited Dominic's next move.

Her muscles coiled tight, ready to spring into action despite her petite frame. She might lack upper-body strength, but determination more than made up for it.

Greer battled conflicting emotions as she watched Dominic delicately picking the lock on the display case. The bait sculpture gleamed under the flickering emergency lights, its porcelain hues sharp against the dim surroundings. Her insides twisted with each subtle sound of Dominic's tools at work.

"Ready?" she breathed, phone shaking in her grip as she dashed off a text to the detective. Alan stood solid beside her. This was it.

Their steps echoed like thunder as they advanced towards Dominic, his every movement calculated and tense. With bated breath, they emerged from hiding just as Dominic lifted the statue from its stand.

"Planning to take that somewhere?" Greer's voice sliced through the silence, strong and commanding, though her nerves threatened to betray her. She channeled her best impression of her stern anthropology professor, though her pulse hammered so hard she could barely hear her own words.

Dominic whirled around, panic flashing in his eyes, his grip slipping on the statue. Alan's swift reflexes saved it from crashing to the ground.

"Easy there," Alan cautioned sharply, his eyes flashing with determination. "That's worth more than your freedom now."

"You don't understand," Dominic spat out bitterly, inching away. The raw desperation in his voice struck a familiar chord. His back collided with a sculpture, sending him reeling against the wall. "I had no choice!"

Greer stepped closer, the weight of months of doubt pressing against her ribs. "Then help me understand, because right now, all I see is a man who knew exactly how to get past our defenses— and broke in to steal from us."

The warning signs had been there from the start. The fresh blue paint slashed across the mural. The clang in the alley. Phoenix's bristled tail. She'd dismissed them as background noise—details unworthy of her time. But they'd all meant something. The story had been unfolding right under her nose, and she hadn't seen it.

Now it was too late to stop the damage, but maybe—just maybe—it wasn't too late to finish the story.

The air crackled with pressure as Dominic struggled to justify his actions while staring down the repercussions of getting caught.

Greer and Alan stood united against deceit, their resolve tested in this critical moment where truth and lies collided, and only time would tell how this high-stakes confrontation would play out next.

Part of her wanted to frame this like a story. But this wasn't a headline—it was a friend on the edge. And she couldn't miss it.

"And when you attacked Alan last month?" Greer's accusation hung heavily in the air, a shard of truth piercing through the tension.

Alan's sharp inhale cut through the charged atmosphere like a blade, the unspoken implications hanging between them like an invisible barrier. Greer flinched at the raw intensity of the moment. She had avoided discussing her suspicions about the incident until now, and Greer's analytical mind whirred with possibilities. Something about Dominic's demeanor had always felt off.

"It was a mistake," Dominic protested weakly, shame coloring his features as guilt etched lines on his face. "He wasn't supposed to be there night."

The nagging feelings reared their ugly heads, triggering the same instincts that had served her well in the past. Her nose for deception never failed her, even if her ability to maintain lasting relation-ships did.

Greer's heart pounded against her ribs as she recognized the reality unfolding before her. "This goes beyond just the artifacts, doesn't it?"

Of course it went deeper. It always did. Her fingers itched for her notebook, wanting to make sure she could recount all the facts later, even as adrenaline coursed through her system.

Her voice held steady despite the turmoil brewing within her. "Stop beating around the bush; what's really going on here?"

Alan moved closer to her side, a subtle gesture of solidarity.

"I'd like some answers too," he interjected sharply, his usual casualness replaced by a steely edge that sent a chill down Greer's spine.

"I didn't plan for any of this to happen!" Dominic's voice lowered as he pushed back against their scrutiny, sweat glistening on his forehead under the dim gallery lights.

Classic guilty behavior. The trembling hands, the excessive perspiration, the defensive posture, all textbook indicators.

"What was the plan then?" Alan demanded.

Dominic's bitter laughter reverberated through

the gallery space, bouncing off marble floors that suddenly felt colder than ever beneath Greer's feet.

Her mouth went dry as she studied him closely. "Who's pulling your strings? Because this elaborate setup…" she gestured towards Dominic's tools and the compromised security system with trembling fingers, "…this isn't something you orchestrated alone."

The strain was palpable as Alan locked eyes with Dominic.

Before Dominic could respond, Phoenix's warning hiss drew their attention to heavy footsteps approaching from the service entrance.

"That would be my associates," Dominic smirked cryptically. "And they're not as forgiving as me." The expected backup seemed to bolster Dominic's arrogance again.

A shared look between Greer and Alan spoke volumes as they braced themselves for the unknown threat looming closer. The air thickened with apprehension as they awaited the arrival of those mysterious associates. Greer's eyes widened as Alan silently nodded towards Dominic, who moved with dangerous precision towards the priceless artifact.

Her nerves kicked into overdrive, tingling with the thrill of catching a thief red-handed. The gallery's air hung heavy with the stench of betrayal as Greer steadied her shaking hands, the hidden camera on her collar recording every moment. Alan's jaw clenched in quiet fury beside her, his gaze unwavering on the unfolding drama before them.

TWENTY-NINE

T hree silhouettes loomed in the entryway, sending a shiver down Greer's spine as childhood memories of shadowy monsters resurfaced. Her thoughts raced to the can of pepper spray nestled in her purse, which was regrettably perched upstairs like every other time she'd found herself in need of defense. Naturally, she'd forgotten it. Apparently, life in a big city still hadn't drilled into her the cardinal rule of survival. Always keep your weapons within reach.

From his concealed perch, Phoenix released another cautionary hiss, mirroring Greer's own trepidation.

"Is there an issue, Dominic?" The voice oozed refinement and femininity, yet carried a chilling familiarity. It dripped with the same condescending inflection Greer had endured from countless high-society women who had sneered at her attire. That tone catapulted her back to her mother-in-law's lavish soirées, where she'd lingered on the fringes, chronicling everyone else's grandeur rather than partaking in it.

Greer's mouth fell agape as Vivian Sinclair emerged into the light, her Louboutin stilettos tapping against the hardwood like an ominous metronome. Those shoes likely surpassed a month of Greer's rent. Not that she was keeping a precise tally.

The Pacific Heights gallery owner appeared strikingly different from their recent encounter in Alan's office. Her designer ensemble remained flaw-less, but a shattered essence lurked behind her eyes, a frantic glint that rendered her more menacing than any run-of-the-mill burglar.

"Ms. Sinclair," Alan's voice quavered with incredulity, his hands quivering at his sides. "You orchestrated this?"

"Please, darling, it's Vivian." She motioned to the two men flanking her, both donning pricey suits that scarcely concealed their sculpted physiques. While the average onlooker might have been duped, Greer's extensive experience at events with bodyguards had honed her ability to detect the subtle protrusion of hidden firearms. Vivian's fingers twitched anxiously, undermining the self-assurance in her voice. "Considering how... intimate we're all becoming."

Despite her pounding heart, Greer's journalistic instincts surged to life, that recognizable rush of adrenaline that had propelled her through countless perilous assignments.

"The rival showcase," Greer said, realization dawning. "At your gallery next month. That's what this little scheme is all about, isn't it?"

Vivian's immaculately groomed eyebrows shot up, but a telltale twitch in her left eye gave her away. "Well, well, the globe-trotting journalist has some bite. Color me surprised." She pivoted to Alan, her smile sharp enough to cut glass. "Oh, your poor father would be positively heartbroken, sweetie. Seeing his precious collection in such a sorry state."

Greer's fingers clenched at the sheer malice dripping from Vivian's words. Years of dealing with shady characters in her previous line of work had given her a nose for deceit, and this woman reeked of it.

"You don't get to talk about my father," Alan

snarled, his voice trembling with barely contained rage and unshed tears. "He saw right through you two decades ago."

"And yet, he could never quite pin anything on me, could he?" Vivian smirked, but her white-knuckled grip on her designer handbag betrayed her unease. "Just like you won't be able to now." She signaled to her henchmen with a curt nod. "Boys, take care of this little mess, won't you?"

Greer found herself caught in a standoff between art thieves and irreplaceable treasures. Her old journalism profs would get a kick out of this one—assuming she lived to file the story.

As the burlier goon advanced on them, Greer's pulse thundered in her ears, a stark reminder of how rapidly this situation could turn deadly. But in a flash of orange fur, Phoenix burst from his hiding spot, leaping onto the pedestal beside Vivian. The one-of-a-kind Murano glass paperweight went flying, shattering on the hardwood with an ear-splitting crash.

Her adorably infuriating feline had just obliterated an object worth more than she made in a year. Still, the sight of Vivian's flawless facade crumbling was almost worth the looming insurance headache.

The ensuing pandemonium would have been

hilarious if Greer's nerves weren't stretched tighter than a high wire. Vivian recoiled with a distinctly inelegant shriek, her manicured hands grasping at thin air. Her suited thugs slammed into each other, expensive loafers grinding the glittering shards into dust. Dominic bolted for the back exit, his frantic footfalls echoing.

"Where the heck are the cops?" Greer muttered through gritted teeth, her mouth drier than the Sahara. "I hit that bloody silent alarm ages ago!" She wiped her sweaty palms on her jeans, silently cursing her decision to wear such impractical pants in a crisis.

A flicker in the gallery lights made her stomach drop. Not the kind caused by faulty wiring—but the kind caused by sabotage. Someone had planned this blackout down to the last second.

Ten minutes crawled by like an eternity when staring down the barrel of an art heist. Sure, she'd faced her fair share of danger—she was a woman, after all—but this was different. This was personal. Alan's gallery, his legacy, his life's work. And she'd dragged him into this mess with her insatiable curiosity and knack for attracting trouble.

Suddenly, the gallery exploded in a kaleidoscope of flashing red and blue lights, bathing everyone's faces in an eerie glow. Vivian's cool composure cracked, a muscle twitching beneath her carefully concealed crow's feet.

"You idiots," she snarled, her manicured fingers curling into talons. "Have you any idea what you've done?"

Greer felt a familiar rush of adrenaline, the exhilaration of defiance temporarily overpowering her pounding heart. Ah, the classic villain monologue. They always got sloppy when they started grandstanding.

"Stopped you from robbing this gallery blind?" Greer quipped, scooping up a smug-looking Phoenix and clutching him close. "Saved Alan's legacy? Ruined your precious Louboutins?"

Phoenix's contented purr rumbled against her chest as she held him, perhaps a bit too tightly. Apparently, her cat had bigger balls than she did. But there wasn't a chance she'd let Vivian see her sweat.

"Oh, you naïve little girl," Vivian laughed, the sound sending shivers down Greer's spine. "Did you really think I'd stay buried in 2004? Death is such an inconvenient label. Better to shed it when it no longer suits. This has always been bigger than a few paintings." She turned to her beefier henchman. "Jorge, take care of these pests. We're done here."

But Jorge remained rooted to the spot, his gaze darting between Vivian and Alan, his Adam's apple bobbing nervously. "I... I can't do it."

"Can't?" Vivian's voice dripped with venom. "Perhaps you need a reminder of our little deal?"

A chink in their armor. Perfect. If Greer could just keep them bickering until the cavalry arrived...

Greer seized the moment, her heart pounding like a jackhammer. "Come on, Jorge, spill the beans. I bet the cops would love to hear all about Vivian's dirty little secrets."

The gallery erupted in pandemonium—Vivian shrieked as Phoenix darted between her heels, sending her sprawling. Her thugs collided with each other, shattering glass underfoot as Alan dragged Greer back.

The wail of sirens swelled, drowning out Vivian's curses. Red and blue light flooded the gallery windows. In an instant, the doors burst open and uniformed officers surged inside, weapons drawn, voices commanding order. Vivian froze, her mask of elegance cracking under the harsh beams of their flashlights. Her muscle dropped their weapons without a fight.

Crime scene techs poured in behind them, brushing past Greer with camera cases and evidence markers, snapping photos and sealing chaos into neat little bags. The air buzzed with radios and shouted commands, but to Greer it all blurred—the only sound that mattered was the thunder of her own pulse.

Then a single voice cut through the noise.

"Enough."

Detective Burman strode into the gallery with the calm assurance of a man who had seen worse and was already two steps ahead. Each purposeful step echoed like a ticking clock, counting down to an inescapable truth. His gaze locked on Vivian. "Vivian Sinclair. Looks like you've finally run out of lives."

Vivian's smirk faltered as the cuffs closed around her wrists. The chaos stilled into an ordered rhythm. For the first time that night, Greer let herself breathe.

With a strangled sigh, Greer prepared for another lecture from the Detective. Something in Burman's demeanor had shifted, a glimpse of genuine concern beneath his typically gruff exterior. The familiar scents of coffee and worn leather permeated the space, adding to the already charged atmosphere as he acknowledged their entanglement in this unfolding drama.

Greer met Burman's gaze. Beside her, Alan's body stiffened.

Burman wasted no time laying out the facts of their predicament, methodically piecing together the puzzle that had eluded Greer until now. Under the harsh light of reality, Alan's bravado crumbled, exposing the fears he'd kept carefully hidden.

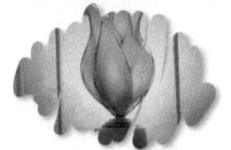

The gallery's eerie silence was shattered when Phoenix chittered and swiped at a banker's box of files tucked under the ominous chair they had been avoiding since they'd first noticed it.

The detective's eyebrow rose as he stared at them for an explanation. Alan looked at her, and she shrugged. Greer hadn't even noticed the box before now.

They peered into the box, the air thickening with anticipation as they grappled with the gravity of their find.

Of course, it would be Phoenix that uncovered the one crucial detail they'd missed. That cat had always possessed an uncanny intuition, even for a creature that spent most of its time lounging in sunbeams and batting at loose threads.

"Ay, Caramba! Alan, look at this!" Greer yanked out a stack of papers, the musty scent of mothballs and long-buried secrets wafting through the air. "These are provenance documents for paintings that disappeared during the war. Check out the dates on these."

Detective Burman stepped closer, his shoulder grazing Alan's as they both leaned in to examine the papers. Neither of them flinched at the proximity. "These records cover the entire World War II era. This is huge."

Greer's mind whirred, the thoughts rearranging themselves in a dizzying new configuration. She'd been so fixated on the present that she'd overlooked the answers buried in the past.

"That's it!" Greer exclaimed, the thrill of discovery sending a jolt of energy through her weary bones. "Alan, could these be the items your grandfather smuggled out of Europe all those years ago?"

The pieces snapped together like a trap slamming shut. This wasn't just about art. It was legacy laundering—an entire history rewritten in museum lighting.

Alan's hands trembled slightly as he gingerly handled the fragile documents. "I can't say for certain, but the timeline definitely fits. My grandfather never spoke much about the war, but I always sensed there was more to the story."

Greer nodded, her head already spinning with the possibilities. This was the break they'd been waiting for, the key to unlocking the truth that had eluded them for so long. But as they stood there, surrounded by the burden of history and the promise of answers, a flicker of unease crept up Greer's spine. They were about to step into uncharted territory, and there was no telling what dangers lay ahead.

"Let me take these documents and have my team dig into them," Detective Burman said, his voice firm but not unkind. "And I need to make that Ms. Sinclair is processed."

Alan reluctantly relinquished the papers, and Burman marched through the gallery, his steps reverberating against the gleaming marble. Greer watched him go, the unforgiving gallery lights casting stark shadows across their faces, exposing the cracks in their composed facades.

Greer shifted uncomfortably, the glare of the lights suddenly too bright, too intrusive. The personal entangled with the professional in a way that defied her fiercely independent nature.

As the door swung shut behind Burman, Greer turned to Alan, her forehead creased with worry. "Did we overstep?" Her words were barely audible, her fingers absently twisting the fabric of her sleeve, a telltale sign of her unease.

Asking for reassurance felt foreign, a vulnerability she typically kept locked away. Her divorce had instilled a deep distrust in her own judgment. But tonight had shaken her to the core, leaving her usual confidence in tatters.

Alan's rings glinted as he waved off her concerns, but Greer noticed the subtle tension in his frame, the way his trademark dramatic flair fell a bit flat. "We did what had to be done, darling. And with our signature panache, I might add."

Her mind whirling, her stomach churning, something kept her rooted in place, perhaps the same tenacious spirit that had fueled her unconventional career path against all odds. Despite the gravity of the situation, a smile tugged at Greer's lips. This wild ride had forged an unexpected connection with Alan, chipping away at the walls she had so carefully erected to shield her heart.

"I guess you're right," she admitted, watching Phoenix contentedly groom himself in the spotlight's warm glow. "But let's not forget the MVP of this operation—our feline super sleuth over here."

Kneeling beside the cat, Greer ran her fingers through his soft fur. Maybe she needed to take a page from Phoenix's book and just wing it.

"Who would've thought our little troublemaker was secretly a detective extraordinaire?" Greer chuckled, a hint of affection coloring her words.

Alan met her gaze with a tenderness that took her aback. "I always had a feeling he was destined for greatness. Though I could've done without the property damage."

"You know," she said, the words tumbling out before she could second-guess herself, "I'm really glad our paths crossed, Alan."

"Well, darling, I am quite the catch," he quipped, his signature bravado resurfacing.

Greer shook her head, but the smile never left her face. For once, she didn't feel the need to hide behind her usual mask of detachment.

As the alarm's wailing finally ceased, an eerie

quiet settled over the gallery, broken only by the sound of their breathing. The sudden stillness felt alien, like stepping into a foreign land without a map. Greer's fingers itched to reach for her journal, to chronicle every twist and turn of this wild ride.

Left alone with their thoughts, the silence grew heavy, weighed down by unspoken fears and lingering questions. Greer's voice cut through the emptiness, echoing off the pristine walls.

"Alan, we've got drugs, stolen art, and now these provenance papers. It feels like we're barely scratching the surface here."

The pieces of the puzzle stubbornly refused to fall into place, defying all of Greer's attempts. Loose threads dangled tantalizingly, each one leading down a different rabbit hole of possibilities. It was like trying to navigate a labyrinth of unnamed streets in a foreign city without a map.

"Greer, I swear, these past few months have been like living in a telenovela," Alan quipped, his voice tinged with exasperation.

Greer chuckled. "Wow, way to date yourself. But you're right, there's no way all of this is a coincidence."

The sound of slow, deliberate clapping echoed through the gallery, causing Greer's shoulders to tense up. Charles Henderson stepped out of the shadows in the corner of the back room, his bespoke Italian suit immaculate as always.

"Bravo, Miss Caldwell. You're getting warmer, but you're still not seeing the big picture."

THIRTY-ONE

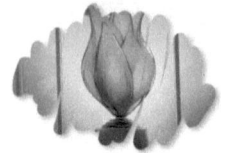

Greer's breath caught in her chest, warning bells ringing in her head. Of course, Henderson would make such a dramatic entrance–he probably rehearsed it in the mirror beforehand. But there was something about his stance, the predatory way he moved, that set her pulse racing.

The mere sight of Henderson sent a chill crawling up the back of Greer's neck, her throat tightening as every instinct screamed danger. The man who claimed to be "like family" to Alan stood before them, a calculating grin plastered across his face. His eyes gleamed with a malevolence that went beyond mere hatred. It was the cold, unwavering certainty of someone accustomed to getting what they wanted, no matter the price.

"The art was never the actual target," Greer breathed, the realization slamming into her like a freight train. "It was the gallery all along."

The truth hit her with the force of an avalanche, everything falling into place with sickening clarity. All those pointed questions Henderson had asked, his ability to always be around just when Alan needed him over the months. She should have seen the pattern sooner. She'd spent enough time with vengeful subjects to recognize when someone was gathering ammunition.

Henderson's smile was devoid of warmth, but his hands trembled slightly. "Giuseppe built this gallery on my family's land. Land stolen from us in the crash. Your precious family legacy is nothing but a house of cards, built on a foundation of theft."

Alan's voice faltered, his face ashen as he gripped the display case for support. "That's bullshit. My grandfather was a good man. Taking advantage like that wasn't in his nature."

Henderson's mask of composure cracked, revealing the raw anguish beneath. "Good? He swooped in like a vulture, snatching up our property for a fraction of its worth. Just like he did with all that art from desperate families fleeing the war. He left us with nothing." Decades of festering bitterness seeped into each word.

"No, you're twisting things. Grandfather helped those families. He protected their treasures," Alan argued, but even he could hear the doubt creeping into his voice. Greer understood how memories of his grandfather's stories would now feel tainted, seen through a darker lens.

Greer could practically see Alan's worldview splintering before her eyes.

Henderson barked a harsh laugh. "Protected? More like profited. But I've been reclaiming what's rightfully ours, piece by piece. And in mere minutes, this whole fucking building will be nothing but rubble. Poetic justice, isn't it? The great Giuseppe's legacy reduced to dust."

Greer gulped. Henderson hadn't just come to destroy a building—he'd come to destroy Alan's family legacy.

The air in the gallery's storage room was thick with the weight of the past. Alan met Henderson's gaze, his voice steady despite the tempest raging within him. "If you had a score to settle with my family, you should have come directly to me. My staff had no part in any of this."

Henderson's smug grin didn't quite reach his eyes, his fingers tapping an anxious rhythm against his thigh. "What's the matter, Alan? Cat got your tongue? Or did daddy dearest not let you in on the family secrets?"

The seconds ticked by, each one ratcheting up the tension. Henderson's tell betrayed a trace of uncertainty, a hairline crack in his vengeful facade. Greer sensed an opening, a fleeting chance to defuse the situation before it spiraled further.

She stepped forward, her heart hammering against her ribs. "Mr. Henderson, I understand your anger, but this isn't the way. Innocent people could get hurt. Is that really what you want?"

As if on cue, Phoenix sprang into action, a blur of fur and claws hurtling towards Henderson with a banshee-like screech. The sudden assault caught Henderson off guard, sending him stumbling backwards.

"Alan, now!" Greer yelled, lunging for the detonator that had slipped from Henderson's grasp. Alan's hand slammed against the evacuation alarm, the shrill sound pulsating through the gallery.

Henderson scrambled to his feet, his once-immaculate suit now a rumpled mess. He made a desperate grab for the detonator, but Greer snatched it away, her fingers curling around the device like a lifeline.

This was definitely not how she'd envisioned her Thursday playing out. Thwarting an unhinged art thief with a penchant for explosives? Just another day in the life of Greer Caldwell, apparently. So much for a quiet week of gallery events and writing deadlines.

Detective Burman burst into the room, his movements precise and practiced. In a flash, he had Henderson pinned to the ground, cuffs snapping into place. "Charles Henderson, you're under arrest. You have the right to remain silent."

As the adrenaline ebbed, the absurdity of the situation overwhelmed Greer. They'd been dodging danger at every turn, only to face their greatest threat from someone she would never have expected.

"Heavens to Betsy, that racket!" Alan exclaimed, his grin not quite concealing the haunted look in his eyes. "Though I must say, the threat of imminent structural collapse adds a certain *je ne sais quoi* to the entire scene, don't you think?"

Trust Alan to find the silver lining in potential

demolition. Greer made a mental note to thank him later for maintaining his signature flair in the face of disaster.

Uniformed officers swarmed the gallery, leading a handcuffed Henderson away. His shoulders slumped, the consequence of his failed vengeance bearing down on him.

Greer stood in the middle of the wreckage, her arms crossed, eyes on the broken frames and ruined canvas. Phoenix trotted up beside her, sniffed the air, then sat on high alert, ears perked.

"You knew something was off," she murmured. "Back in the alley. I should've listened."

Phoenix let out a low huff, as if to say, *finally*.

Greer smiled—not the tired, hollow kind she'd worn for weeks, but something steadier.

She crouched next to him, resting a hand on his warm back.

"Next time," she whispered, "we follow your instincts first."

And this time, she meant it.

CHAPTER

THIRTY-TWO

Greer knew she should feel relieved, but mostly she just felt numb. And ravenous. Nothing worked up an appetite quite like a brush with death. Pad Thai sounded heavenly right about now. But that would have to wait.

Later, huddled in Alan's office, wrapped in shock blankets, he pressed a mug of his "emergency chamomile tea" into her hands. Greer snorted. The electric kettle in his office was certainly coming in handy now.

"Darling, a proper cup of tea is essential in times of crisis," Alan said, his hands trembling slightly as he poured another mug.

Detective Burman accepted the offered tea, his

gaze lingering on Alan. "What's so amusing?" he asked.

"Just thinking about my old travel blog motto," she said, scratching Phoenix's ears and drawing comfort from his warm presence. "'The best stories are found in the footnotes.' Never thought it would become my sleuthing catchphrase."

Her fingers shook as she stroked Phoenix's fur. This was nothing like exploring ancient temple passages or unearthing forgotten village traditions. Actual lives had been at stake here, not just looming article deadlines.

Detective Burman cleared his throat. "Speaking of footnotes, forensics found detailed records of Henderson's family history on Vivian Sinclair's phone. Looks like he's been plotting this revenge for decades."

A nagging suspicion gnawed at Greer, the same relentless instinct that compelled her to triple-check every detail before embarking on a new adventure. The timeline was inconsistent, and her journalist's intuition warned her that a crucial piece of the puzzle was still missing. It was like setting off on a trek without a compass, and Greer hated feeling unprepared.

Alan's voice pulled her from her thoughts. "You

know, I always thought the biggest threat to the gallery was Marco's inability to arrange a display without causing a minor catastrophe." He aimed for levity, but the slight tremor in his words betrayed the stress that had haunted him these past weeks. The terrifying possibility of losing not only the gallery, but the very dream he'd poured his heart into.

"Watch it!" Greer yelped, narrowly dodging the crumpled napkin Alan lobbed her way. She tucked her shaking hands beneath her thighs, hoping to hide her own unease. "Hey, at least my borderline obsessive attention to detail finally paid off. That, and Phoenix's impeccable taste in footwear."

Detective Burman reached over, helping Alan straighten his disheveled scarf. The gallery's lights caught the concern in his eyes. "Well, I guess this explains why you two have a knack for turning up at my crime scenes."

Greer stifled a sarcastic retort. Leave it to Burman to make it sound like they were actively seeking trouble, as if murder mysteries were just another item on their daily agenda, sandwiched between gallery events and looming deadlines.

"Oh, please," Alan scoffed, falling back on their familiar banter like a lifeline. "It's not our fault your crime scenes have a habit of spilling over into my gallery. And while we're on the subject of spilling…" He shot Burman a pointed look, grateful for the way their usual back-and-forth made the world feel a little more stable. "I believe you owe me dinner, detective. Or did you forget our little wager about Marco's involvement in all this?"

Greer felt things shift in the bubble she'd been living in as she watched Alan and Detective Burman's awkward dance around their obvious attraction become her favorite distraction from the dumpster fire that was her own love life. At least someone might get a happily ever after out of this mess.

As the unlikely pair walked out of the room, the detective's jacket draped over Alan's shoulders like a racy romance novel cover, Greer smiled. The comforting scent of oil paint and canvas enveloped her, a reminder that despite the chaos, the gallery remained a sanctuary.

Phoenix leaped into her lap, his throaty purrs resonating on her. The simple act of petting him grounded her, the lingering adrenaline from their brush with danger slowly ebbing away.

But even as a sense of normalcy settled over the gallery, Greer couldn't escape the nagging feeling that something still didn't quite add up. Call it journalistic instinct or just plain paranoia, but those unanswered questions buzzed within her thoughts like an angry hornet's nest. She'd learned the hard way to trust her gut, even if it meant sacrificing sleep and sanity to chase down leads.

"Guess I'm just a nosy travel writer who doesn't know when to quit," she muttered. "By the way—what's the deal with that barista across the street?"

Phoenix's tail twitched, his golden eyes narrowing as if to say, "I'm on it, boss."

Greer hugged him closer, drawing strength from his unwavering loyalty. The case might be closed on paper, but her instincts warned her the actual story had only just begun. Shadows lurked beneath the surface, secrets waiting to be dragged into the unforgiving light of truth. And if there was one thing Greer Caldwell excelled at, it was shining a spotlight on the things people desperately wanted to keep hidden.

THIRTY-THREE

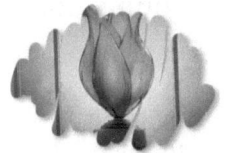

T *wo weeks later*

THREE MONTHS AND TWELVE DAYS HAD PASSED SINCE Greer took that life-changing leap of faith and moved to San Francisco. The memory of her arrival was vivid as she maneuvered through the labyrinth of unpacked boxes, the echoes of her tearful nights a constant companion.

Perched by the window, the city's skyline sparkling, Greer's fingers absentmindedly stroked Phoenix's back, unspooling the memories etched into her very being. The aroma of fried rice was a bittersweet reminder of her past victories and defeats.

An unseen cord bound her to the past, loneliness creeping at the fringes of her mind. Eyes closed, she let the haunting thoughts wash over her.

Greer reached for the time-worn framed photo on the windowsill, the image a testament to her vulnerability and resilience. As her fingers grazed the edges, a surge of determination flooded through her veins. Despite the hardships, she was here to stay.

"You know," she murmured, "when I first got here, I was scared to death. I called my sister that first night, the fog rolling in, blanketing the strange streets, wondering if I'd ever find my place."

Alan glanced up from his book, eyebrows arched. "Seriously? You seemed like you had it all together, fearless as all get out."

Greer laughed. "I tried to be what you needed. Isn't it funny how we both put on a brave face for each other?"

"And here we are," Alan said, his thumb drawing circles on his wrist. "Two beautiful train wrecks who found a home in each other's fractured pieces."

The remark struck her like a glass of cold water

over her head. Beautiful train wrecks. That's exactly what they were, weren't they? A travel writer wrestling with social anxiety and her larger-than-life art dealer roommate, stitching together their own patchwork family. Greer's gaze wandered back to the San Francisco skyline, the lights smudging through the sudden veil of tears.

"You know what terrifies me sometimes? How much this all means now. How much you both mean to me." Her voice caught on the last word, exposing the raw emotion, the vulnerability she usually kept under lock and key.

"Oh, honey," Alan's voice wavered, his own eyes shimmering in the dim light. "You're stuck with us now. As scary as that might be. We're sure as heck not going anywhere."

Phoenix chose that exact moment to stretch languidly, his claws flexing as he shifted positions. The mischievous feline nearly tumbled off her lap, eliciting a burst of laughter from Greer; the sound held a hint of hysteria. Leave it to the cat to defuse an emotional moment with his impeccable comic timing. Their shared mirth broke through the heavy atmosphere, dispelling the tension, though the tell-tale sheen of unshed tears still glistened in their eyes.

"And you, Mr. Trouble," Greer playfully chided the cat, swiping at her eyes with the back of her hand, "you're the little fuzzy glue that keeps us all together. What in the world would we do without you?"

The words stuck in her throat, thick with an emotion she seldom permitted herself to confront. It was funny, really, how this orange tabby had wormed his way past her meticulously constructed walls of independence.

While the movie played on, black and white images flickering across the screen, Greer felt that familiar warmth blooming in her chest. But now, it carried their shared confessions, their matched vulnerabilities. Here, nestled on the couch with her best friend and their beloved cat, she'd stumbled upon something she never realized she'd been missing all along, a place where she could be both beautifully broken and wholly cherished, a home built on the foundations of honesty and acceptance.

The realization struck her with startling clarity. She'd spent years watching the lives of others, when her own story had been patiently waiting to unfold. Her greatest adventure would be learning to stay still and letting someone else share her space, her heart.

Greer chuckled, though it came out a bit shakier than intended. "Trust me, it was all an act. I was so convinced I'd crash and burn at Epic Destinations. When I was a project manager, I used to practice conversations in the bathroom mirror before team meetings, just so I wouldn't stumble over my words. I'd pace back and forth, rehearsing my lines until they sounded natural, until I could say them without my voice shaking like a leaf."

That old life? Gone. She'd clawed her way into this world, every story a tightrope walk. But this— this felt like flying blind.

"And let's not forget my new role as a feline behavior expert," Greer chuckled, as Phoenix playfully swatted at her hand, his contented purrs vibrating against her palm. "In all seriousness, I never thought I'd feel this... grounded. At least, most of the time." She paused, her throat constricting with a sudden swell of emotion. "There are still mornings when I wake up, half-expecting to find myself back in that lonely house, drowning in a sea of unrealistic expectations."

Alan tilted his head, his brows knitting together in contemplation. "So, what do you think was the turning point? What made the difference for you?"

Greer took a moment to gather her thoughts,

the distant cry of a foghorn weaving through the open window, harmonizing with the soft whisper of leaves in the night air. "I suppose… I finally learned to embrace the unexpected. To approach the world with a sense of curiosity, even when it pushed me out of my comfort zone."

"Ah, like playing amateur detective and unraveling the mystery of those art heists?" Alan grinned, a mischievous twinkle in his eye.

"Precisely," Greer beamed, her face aglow with newfound excitement. "I never imagined that cracking cases could be such a thrill. It's opened my eyes to the fact that adventure is hiding around every corner, just waiting to be discovered. Even something as simple as stumbling upon that charming French bakery down the street, the one where the owner always has a chocolate croissant set aside for me on Sundays, greeting me with a warm smile and remembering my regular order. It's those small gestures of belonging that hold so much meaning now."

"And taking those leaps of faith, stepping outside your usual boundaries," Alan remarked, nodding in understanding.

Greer sighed, her gaze turning introspective as she absently fiddled with a loose thread on the sleeve of her sweater. "That's been the most challenging aspect, if I'm being honest. Daring myself to embrace new experiences even when every fiber of my being is urging me to play it safe. But it's also been the most fulfilling. I've uncovered facets of myself I never knew were there."

"Such as your secret gift for communicating with felines?" Alan teased, nodding towards Phoenix, who was now curled up in Greer's lap, fast asleep, his whiskers twitching as he nestled into the cozy fabric of her sweater.

"Oh, stop it, you," Greer laughed, giving him a playful whack with a plush velvet pillow, the soft material grazing his shoulder. "But you're right, even about that. It's the little unanticipated delights that make life so rich, you know? The surprises that catch you unawares and force you to see the world through a different lens."

As the movie's end credits scrolled across the screen, Greer reached for the remote and clicked off the TV. She turned to Alan, one eyebrow arched in an unspoken query.

Alan's expression softened, his eyes brimming with warmth. "I do know. And I'm ecstatic that you've found a sense of belonging here, with us.

That you've carved out a home in this city, in this beautiful, messy, wonderful life of mine."

Greer swallowed at a lump forming as she blinked back the sudden sting of tears. The city lights blurred, twinkling like distant stars through the watery veil. "Me too," she managed, her voice cracking under the weight of her confession. "More than words can express."

"All right, sleepyheads, time to shake a leg!" Alan announced, springing to his feet with an exaggerated stretch, his joints cracking in protest. He extended a hand to Greer, wiggling his fingers invitingly. "We've got a soirée to prep for, and those canapés won't arrange themselves."

CHAPTER

THIRTY-FOUR

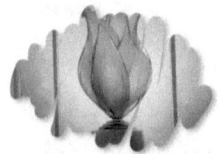

G reer's brow furrowed, a flicker of uncertainty crossing her features. "Soirée? I thought you said it was just a small get-together." Her fingers absently curled into Phoenix's fur, eliciting a disgruntled mew from the drowsy feline. Realizing her mistake, she quickly loosened her grip, soothing the cat with gentle strokes. "Seriously, how many people are we talking about here?"

"Oh, you know, just a cozy little gathering," Alan replied breezily, waving a dismissive hand. But Greer caught the mischievous glint in his eye, the subtle quirk of his lips that betrayed his nonchalance.

Greer heaved a sigh, resigning herself to the

inevitable. She could handle a handful of guests, couldn't she? As if fate had a twisted sense of humor, she'd chosen to live above an art gallery, a haven for a self-professed introvert who found solace in the company of well-worn journal pages and dog-eared travel guides. Yet somehow, Alan had coaxed her out of her shell, gradually expanding her social circle, one charming acquaintance at a time. The constant stream of visitors to the gallery caught her off guard, a stark contrast to her meticulously curated solitude. Blending into the background had become second nature. But anonymity was a rare commodity when your roommate was the life of every party in the city. Maybe, just maybe, this was another chance to discover hidden depths within herself.

The living room glowed invitingly, bathed in the warm ambiance of twinkling fairy lights. Greer chewed at the edge of her lip, itching to reach for her laptop and lose herself in a rabbit hole of obscure research topics. She surveyed the room, taking in the animated chatter and clinking glasses, a bittersweet mix of contentment and that all-too-familiar pang of loneliness. It was oddly poetic, feeling more at ease amidst the chaotic bustle of a foreign market than at this intimate gathering. These moments always stirred up old memories, reminders of a life spent on the periphery, bearing witness to the joys and sorrows of others while keeping her own story firmly under wraps.

"Can you believe we actually pulled this off?" Greer marveled, watching Alan meticulously arrange the hors d'oeuvres platter with the same precision he'd used to piece together his gallery downstairs. Looking at him now, his brow furrowed in concentration as he positioned each canapé just so. A wave of affection washed over her for this man. "From cracking art heists to throwing fancy parties, I've come a long way, haven't I?"

Alan looked up, flashing her a dazzling grin that never failed to make her heart flutter, though she noticed the slight fidgeting of his hands. "Darling, we're an unstoppable duo. Now, be a love and keep Kyle's glass topped up tonight. Something tells me he might need a bit of liquid courage."

Greer's eyebrow shot up, intrigued. Something was definitely percolating beneath Alan's flamboyant veneer. The subtle quiver in those bejeweled fingers spoke volumes. Plus, "liquid courage" coming from Alan usually signaled either impending disaster or matchmaking shenanigans.

She leaned in, lowering her voice conspiratori-ally. "Oh, really? And why might that be?"

Before Alan could reply, the doorbell chimed, reverberating through the apartment. Greer went to answer it, revealing Detective Kyle Burman looking endearingly out of place in a crisp polo. That vulnerable uncertainty, the way he fidgeted from foot to foot.

It was all making sense now. Alan's jittery energy, Kyle's uncharacteristically casual attire... Question was, did they even realize what they were doing?

"Detective! So glad you made it," Greer greeted warmly, even as her heart clenched with a tangled mix of joy and trepidation for her friend, for the gamble he was taking by opening himself up to the possibility of connection... and heartache.

She made a silent vow to keep a watchful eye, to stay vigilant for any signs of either man backpedal-ing. After all, looking out for Alan was practically written into her lease agreement, unofficial adden-dum, page one.

"Thanks for the invite," Burman said, his grav-elly voice imbued with a hint of warmth. He extended a bottle of wine, the label partially concealed by his broad hand. "Wasn't sure what to bring, so I went with a classic red. Hope that works."

As Greer welcomed him inside, she caught the faint blush spreading across the detective's neck, the way his eyes kept flicking to Alan as if drawn by an invisible force. Her instincts clicked on, dissecting glances and posture like a seasoned observer. This wasn't just small talk—it was the beginning of something raw.

"Kyle, don't you clean up nice," Alan remarked, his tone uncharacteristically tender. He accepted the proffered wine, his fingers grazing Kyle's in the exchange. "So, red or white? Name your poison, and I'll make it happen."

THIRTY-FIVE

An unfamiliar surge of peace swelled in Greer's chest. She'd watch for every potential red flag, every warning sign—a reflexive response honed by years of observing from a safe distance. But something told her this connection had been a lifetime in the making.

"Red sounds perfect," Burman replied, a gentle smile playing at the corners of his mouth. "I seem to recall you have a weakness for it." He adjusted his stance, the tension easing from his shoulders as he took in the inviting ambiance of the apartment, the soothing murmur of voices.

Greer's brows lifted, and she stifled a knowing smirk, even as a twinge of protective concern tugged at her heart. She'd become adept at reading between the lines, at detecting the imperceptible tremors that foreshadowed emotional upheavals. The detective's attentiveness set off alarms—not because he appeared disingenuous, but because he seemed almost too good to be true. Like a fractured vase restored with precious metal, the scars had rendered him more exquisite, but no less fragile. The haunted look that shadowed his eyes even in moments of laughter.

As the evening unfolded, Greer found herself entranced by the intricate ballet between Alan and Detective Burman. It was there in the stolen glances, the accidental brush of hands reaching for the same hors d'oeuvre, the inside jokes that had them both chuckling like old friends. She could see the first tender shoots of something beautiful, the hesitant bloom of possibility.

"Well, I'll be darned," Greer mumbled, a bittersweet warmth spreading through her chest, with a pang of jealousy she instantly regretted. "Alan deserves someone who gets how fabulous he is. Who would've guessed it'd be Mr. By-the-Book detective?" Thinking back to that first meeting with Burman, the way he'd rolled his eyes at Alan's dramatic flair, the doubt written all over his rugged face. It was clear this was different for both of them, something deeper, more real.

Greer drifted to the window as the party buzzed on, observing their guests with a cocktail of happiness and melancholy. The city lights twinkled hazily through the glass, blurring the lines between solitude and togetherness, between watcher and participant. The soft scuff of shoes made her turn to find Alan at her side, curiosity and concern mingling in his gaze as he cocked his head, trying to puzzle out her thoughts like he often did.

"Alright, spill. What's on your mind, gorgeous?" His voice was gentle, the question wrapped in memories of countless heart-to-hearts over late-night tea and cozy blankets.

That familiar phrase cocooned her like a favorite sweater. Heavens, in the last few months, how many nights had they whiled away just like this, trading secrets and pipe dreams? Somewhere along the line, Alan had become as vital as her daily caffeine fix, as soothing as Phoenix's contented purrs against her shins.

Greer bumped him playfully, relishing the plush cashmere of his sweater. "Oh, nothing much. Just... reflecting on how far we've come. And how some things are different now." The words didn't quite capture the whirlwind inside her, the sweet ache of watching your person inch towards their own bliss, knowing it means releasing them.

Her throat closed traitorously. Different. Even the idea sent little zings of unease through her ribs. She'd made a career of chasing the new and unfamiliar, but watching Alan dive into romance made her want to cling to their safe, comfortable habits like a kid with a ratty teddy bear. Pretty lame considering she should be popping champagne, not battling the stupid impulse to lock their cozy twosome in a time capsule.

Alan's eyes followed hers to where Kyle was holding court, hands flying, face glowing as he raved about Alan's recent shenanigans. "Guess life's just full of curveballs, huh?" He sounded equal parts giddy and guarded. The thrill of fresh starts all tangled up with the bruises from past hurts.

The excitement and uncertainty in Alan's voice echoed Greer's own jumbled feelings, a potent mix of fierce protectiveness and genuine happiness. Protective instinct surged. What if this ended badly? What if Alan's safe space shattered? She bit back the fear. Not tonight.

"Ain't that the truth?" Greer's words were laced with affection and the faintest hint of tears. She turned to face Alan head-on, instinctively reaching out to pick at nonexistent lint, a gesture as natural as breathing. "And I couldn't be happier for you, Alan. You deserve every bit of joy this world offers." Her voice wavered slightly, thick with the depth of her love for this man who had become her chosen family.

Alan's face softened, and he gave her hand a reassuring squeeze, reading the unspoken fears in her eyes, the silent vow to be his safety net if he stumbled. "So do you, my dear friend. So do you." His gaze held a fierce tenderness, a reminder that their friendship was the unshakeable foundation upon which everything else was built.

Those simple words struck Greer with unexpected intensity. She had spent countless years keeping people at a safe distance, shielding herself from the sting of disappointment. Yet somehow, this vibrant, larger-than-life gallery owner had slipped past her carefully constructed barriers, bringing with him a found family she never had even while she was married to Peter.

A profound sense of belonging washed over Greer, intertwined with the bittersweet realization that all relationships come with rewards and risks. San Francisco, with its thriving art scene and quirky neighborhoods, had evolved into more than just another city to explore for her writing. It had become home, with all the intricacies and vulnerabilities that entailed. In this city of fog-shrouded secrets and hidden delights, she had finally discovered a place to sink her roots deep, to create a life overflowing with laughter, tears, and love in all its glorious forms.

Greer's gaze drifted back to the party, to the sight of Kyle animatedly chatting with a group of Alan's artist friends, his face alight with a boyish enthusiasm. The detective seemed to sense her scrutiny, glancing up and catching her eye. He raised his glass in a silent toast, a lopsided grin forming.

"Well, would you look at that," Alan murmured, a note of awe in his voice. "Our dear detective is full of surprises tonight."

Greer chuckled, bumping her shoulder against Alan's. "Looks like we both are, huh? Embracing the unexpected, taking a chance on something new and terrifying and wonderful all at once."

Alan draped an arm around her shoulders, pulling her close. "Ain't that the truth, gorgeous? Here's to taking leaps of faith and building a beautiful, messy, imperfect life."

As they clinked their glasses, the crystal chiming

like bells, Greer couldn't shake the feeling that this moment marked the start of a thrilling new chapter filled with art heists and found families, laughter and love. And for once, she was ready to dive in headfirst, no matter where the currents might take her.

To find more books by Dawn M. Baca:
books2read.com/dawnmbaca
To find more books by Dawn Baca:
books2read.com/dawnbaca
To join my newsletter:
Dawnbaca.com

ACKNOWLEDGMENTS

Every book is an adventure. Some more than others. Especially when you change genres and write in a whole new world.

I will forever be grateful for my coach, Scarlett Moss, for nudging me in this direction. And to Nellie Steele and Sherry Soule for all your support in learning to write my first mystery. It has been a wild ride, opening my arms and spreading my wings.

To my amazing beta readers, critique partners and editors, some, who are not only fantastic friends but also amazing authors in their own right:

Roxx T. at Proof Perfect, Caroline Trunoske, Jacqueline Clemens, Deb Julienne, Emilee Beck, Lorraine Upton, Michon Franssen, and Rachel Lamb. Without you, none of this would be possible.

Thanks,
Dawn

ABOUT THE AUTHOR

An insatiable reader of all genres since her childhood, Dawn is a globetrotter hungry to discover new places and experience unique adventures.

She can be found indulging in her husband's first love of summer camping in the mountains or luxuriating in the open seas while cruising to exotic destinations during the frigid winter months.

When she's not jet-setting she can be found in Central Valley California with her family and their many rescue animals.

To read her blog, get the latest news, future release dates, or to join her ARC team sign up for her newsletter at *www.DawnBaca.com*.

Social Media

- facebook.com/DawnMBaca
- x.com/BacaDawn
- instagram.com/dawnbaca
- bsky.app/profile/BacaDawn
- tiktok.com/@bacadawn
- youtube.com/DawnBaca
- pinterest.com/dawnmbaca
- amazon.com/author/dawnbaca
- bookbub.com/profile/dawn-baca
- goodreads.com/dawnbaca